Lady Beverley's Redemption

Lady Beverley's Redemption

Jan Farstad

Lady Beverley's Redemption

© Jan Farstad 2018

This book is a work of fiction. Named locations are used fictitiously, and characters and incidents are the product of the author's imagination. Any resemblance to actual events or places or persons, living or dead, is entirely coincidental.

Published by
Lighthouse Christian Publishing
SAN 257-4330
5531 Dufferin Drive
Savage, Minnesota, 55378
United States of America

www.lighthousechristianpublishing.com

PROLOGUE

Lord Burnside had wrestled with a most perplexing dilemma for three long weeks. He dropped his pen in the holder and blotted the ledger, satisfied that his estate was in order. He bowed his head and offered up a silent prayer requesting confirmation that he had made the best decision. In the end, he decided to spare his daughter the burden of knowing that it was unlikely he would live more than a few weeks. He drew comfort knowing that God would direct the world even after he was gone.

He wondered if perhaps the Lord would give him a few more months in spite of the brutally honest words of the heart specialist who had discouraged the idea and frankly told him to put his house in order. It would be sudden and quite painless, the man promised.

Thomas Murray, Lord Burnside, had made peace with his Maker and was quite certain that his only child, Bevie, and young William Henderson would soon make a fine match. He took a small sip of his coffee, leaned back in his chair, fell asleep, and was gone.

CHAPTER ONE

England 1857

Lady Beverley stood perfectly still with her head tilted upward. "Did you hear a gunshot?" she asked her maid, Suzie.

"I didn't hear nuthin' like it, miss. Which gown do you want today?"

Lady Beverley pulled aside the curtains and looked out over the green lawns and wooded acres that surrounded the vast estate. "I'm sure I heard something. I have a strange feeling something awful has happened."

"Everything is fine, miss. Come now and have your bath."

"Are you certain you heard nothing untoward, Suzie?"

"Yes, miss."

"Oh very well, perhaps it was my imagination. I believe I shall wear the new pink chambray. No, no, I prefer to save that for a more festive occasion. The green one with the flowered edge will do for an unbearably boring tea with William's family."

"Yes, miss."

"Don't shoot again, William! Point that weapon to the ground. I do not wish to be a victim of your infernal stupidity," charged Bain Henderson, Viscount Sedley, who was weary of trying to teach his nephew and heir to function with some semblance of responsibility. "Good grief, William, have a care. Do make some attempt to think twice before firing the gun in such close proximity to the neighbor's home."

"They do have an abundance of game ready for the taking and we are hunting rabbits, are we not, Uncle?"

"Indeed, but we are not yet in desperate need of food. You forget that Burnside has not invited us to hunt on his land. Luck has avoided us today, but perhaps we shall fare much better tomorrow when we take the dogs behind the copse on the other side of our stables. Come along now."

"There's a fat one. Allow me to take it down and then we will be off for home."

"No, William!"

Nevertheless, William shot at the animal and missed once again.

Viscount Sedley tore the gun from his nephew's hands. "You dunderhead," he exclaimed through his clenched teeth. "I told you to stop this nonsense! I believe I just heard the pop of broken glass. We had better investigate the matter and determine what damage you've done this time. Burnside will undoubtedly require me to pay double for the repairs to his home."

They ambled along the cobblestone path to the inlaid-brick terrace and stopped in front of the glass doors that led into the library of Thomas Murray, Fifth Earl of Burnside.

"Look there, William, there's a bullet hole just above the handle. We should go around to the front entrance and offer to replace the glass."

"Oh come now, Uncle, they will hardly notice the small hole for a week or two."

"Perhaps you have the right of it. Your aunt is expecting us for tea and she will not take kindly to our tardiness. In fact, I believe she has invited Burnside's girl – Beverley, is it? That should make you eager to return to the house for tea."

"Anyone can see that Bevie is a beauty, Uncle, but she has cut me on several occasions and I cannot countenance her snide remarks."

"Stand still one moment, William. I distinctly thought I heard someone running through the garden path."

"It was only the rabbits dashing away for fear of coming to our dinner table."

"Indeed. Let us hurry before we are soaked to the core."

Bevie heaved a big sigh as her maid tugged on the strings of her stays. "How am I to eat when there is no room for the food to pass through my pipes? Do ease the laces a bit, Suzie."

"Yes, miss," her maid responded dutifully as she yanked harder on the cords and tied them.

"I detest going to Viscount Sedley's home. His wife is nearly always hysterical and she never ceases to foist her nephew off on me. William is a goose and I loathe the way he stares at me and dresses the part of a dandy."

"I know you do, miss."

"Do not dare mention to Father that I said as much, Suzie. He is lately in favor of a match between us. He and Lord Sedley are fast friends and I am fearful the two men will try to force the marriage."

"Of course you are, miss. Let me fix your hair and then you'll be ready to take your leave."

With hair in place, Bevie made her way to the library to inform her father that she had called for the carriage to be brought around since rain was falling steadily. She knocked quietly and when there was no response, she slowly opened the door. "Father, are you in here?"

She entered the room, expecting to see her father with his nose in a book and his mind totally absorbed in whatever he was reading. Instead, she first saw his legs and, as she stepped around the desk, she saw him lying motionless on the floor with blood seeping from a head wound.

She opened her mouth to scream, but no sound came forth. She tried to run, but her legs would not move. A wave of nausea rushed through her. A curtain of darkness descended around her. She collapsed next to the body, hitting her head on the corner of the desk as she crumbled to the floor.

The two men, one young and one middle-aged, pushed through their neighbor's hedge and walked briskly toward the decaying estate that was their home. Rain began to fall in earnest as they stepped across the threshold into the cold vestibule and proceeded to remove their coats and mud-caked boots. Hearing the scuffling, Carter, the butler, hurried to aid them.

Lady Sedley happened into the hallway, looked at the mess on the floor, and screamed. "I am expecting a guest. How dare you tromp in here with that disgusting filth on your feet."

"Do calm yourself, Margaret. You startle the servants."

"Take those boots outside, both of you!" She ran into the drawing room, murmuring disjointed words between sobs, which amounted to something about having invited Bevie solely for William's sake. A moment later she poked her head into the hallway and calmly stated, "Goodness knows the boy must marry money, Bain."

William and Bain exchanged glances and purposed to look intelligently impressed with her words.

Bain spoke to William in a near whisper. "Tea is in one hour. Might it be possible for you to dress with some decorum today, William? I do not wish to dine with a blasted popinjay sitting at my table."

William, who was generally unaffected by any such comments concerning his personal appearance which he viewed as dashing, took offense at his uncle's insulting remark. He shuffled off toward his room pondering the day when he would inherit his uncle's estate and become his own man.

He lay on his bed thinking earnestly – a rare occurrence. He had just come down from Oxford on holiday and had no intention of returning to that boorish intellectual scene. At any rate, it was inevitable that he would eventually be sent down for failure to perform according to their high standards. He examined several ways of escaping that ineluctable fate without incurring the wrath of his uncle.

He seriously considered marriage. He was quite certain Bevie would agree to have him if he made an effort to treat her with care and act the part of a Corinthian – similar to those young bloods who were forever gathered around and fawning over her like lovesick puppies. Her chestnut hair, blue eyes, and pleasing form attracted an ever-increasing number of suitors.

William sighed, frustrated over the fact that she seldom gave him a second glance, save for the times her cutting remarks flew at him like daggers. He left his bed and dressed in drab colors before he met his family for tea.

Sedley's family and servants postponed their tea well past the appointed time for Bevie's arrival. They discussed possible reasons for her failure to appear. It was finally agreed that she was never tardy and, therefore, had simply forgotten. They decided to take tea without her. Lady Sedley hissed and clucked her tongue in disgust at Bevie's abominable manners and the waste of their fine food. They seldom set such a lavish table since their funds were diminishing.

"I am truly alarmed at the state of our finances, Bain," Lady Sedley whimpered after the few servants they still employed had left the room.

"Do not overset yourself, Margaret. Something will come about to change matters," Bain assured his nervous wife.

William snapped out of his stupor, quickly taking advantage of the conversation. "I, too, have seen the decline in your circumstances, Uncle. Since I am your heir, I am prepared to make a most extreme sacrifice. I shall step down from my studies and prepare to marry someone with a considerable fortune. In that way, we may restore the Sedley name and financial position."

Lady Sedley perked up. "Those were my thoughts exactly, my dear boy. Shall you consider courting Bevie? She is lovely and I have learned that her dowry is enormous."

William feigned surprise. "Truly, Aunt? I had thought the abrasive chit to have a scant dowry. If you are certain about the matter, I shall try to overlook her faults for the sake of our Glenarm Place and the Sedley name."

Margaret reached over to pat William's hand. A tear rolled down her cheek. "It is wonderful of you to offer to do such a thing, William."

Bain choked on his tea. He seriously doubted that William had a chivalrous bone in his body – or much substance between his ears.

Lord Burnside had left word that he wished to forego tea that day. Nevertheless, his butler, Franklin, knocked on the library door to make certain his employer had not changed his mind. When there was no answer, he cautiously entered the library. The scene before him nearly sent him swooning onto the pile of bodies crumpled on the floor. When he had finally gathered his wits, he swiftly left the room and called for a footman to fetch the constable. He then returned to the scene of the crime and forced his mind to retain as many of the details as his shocked senses would allow.

It was almost a quarter hour before Bevie opened her eyes and stared upward into the face of Franklin. It took her a moment to reconstruct the horror that had sent her into a faint.

"How can this have happened, Franklin?" she asked weakly.

Franklin shook his head. "That is something you will have to explain to Constable Green, Lady Beverley. He is on his way as we speak."

Bevie slowly sat up. When she began to realize the full extent of the situation, she burst into tears. She bent over her father's body and rested her head on his chest. "You cannot leave me, Father."

Franklin pulled her away from her father and led her to a chair on the other side of the library. "Sit down here, miss. This is going to be a very long day. I don't want to call this tragedy to the attention of the rest of the household staff until the constable arrives. Allow me to serve you a small glass of brandy to calm your nerves."

"No, no, Franklin, I don't drink brandy. I cannot understand. I don't want to believe it. Who has done this to Father?"

"I don't want to be brutal, Lady Beverley, but it looks very much like you was the one who done him in," Franklin said, slipping back into his former careless grammar.

Bevie struggled to stay upright in the chair as the room began to spin slowly around. "How can you say such a thing, Franklin?"

Franklin remained silent.

"I believe I will have a glass of brandy," Bevie said as she tried to comprehend the accusation Franklin had pointedly made against her.

Franklin heard a commotion outside the room and went out to await the arrival of the constable. The footman tried to gain entrance to the library, but Franklin blocked his way and told him to tend to his duties and keep his mouth shut.

Constable Green hurriedly greeted Bevie who was still weeping. He walked around the room and appeared to take in each and every detail before he directed a question toward Bevie.

"Were you present at the time of Lord Burnside's demise?"

Bevie explained how she had come into the room and found her father on the floor.

"How is it that the butler found you lying beside the body, miss?"

She stammered in nervous confusion as she told him how she had fainted at the sight of her father. Even as she spoke, it began to dawn on her that she was considered a suspect in the death of her own father.

"Why would anyone think I did this to Father, Constable Green? I loved him and he was all the family I had."

"We shall certainly endeavor to obtain the answers to those questions," he said coldly. "My men will be here shortly and my detective will undoubtedly want to question you further. We will have the body removed to the morgue in due time, but I will have to ask you to remain in the house until my men have completed their investigation."

Bevie was in such a state of turmoil that she had no idea what to do. She had no one to whom she could turn and she had never dealt with the details of a death in the family. Her mother had passed on when she was a baby. Her only relatives were distant ones whom she had seen once or twice during her twenty years. Her governess had long since departed for another position.

She waited in agony and disbelief as a hoard of men searched through her father's belongings and forced her to answer questions, the subject matter of which she had no knowledge. When at last they excused her, she went to her room and collapsed on her bed. She hoped upon hope that she would awaken from the nightmare. The hands on her clock appeared to stand still. She rang for her maid, Suzie, who came at once.

"I heard a ruckus below and a lot of men is goin' in and out of here, miss. What happened?" Suzie asked.

Bevie began to sob. "Oh Suzie, I don't know what to do. I feel so helpless. My father is dead and they believe I killed him."

Suzie stood motionless, momentarily stunned into silence. Presently, she whispered, "Did you, miss?"

Her question brought on louder sobbing. "How could you ask such a thing? You know how I admired my father."

"Tell me about what happened. I grew up on the streets and I seen too much for one person to see, but I knowed the ways of the world and mayhap I can help you know what to do."

Bevie related the horror of finding her father in the library. "I fainted and hit my head on his desk. Franklin found me lying on the floor next to my father and he thinks I killed him."

"Let me have a look at yer head. Well, you got a gash there and a bump. I'll get something to fix it up."

"Don't leave me, Suzie. I'm very frightened."

"I'll go and find Mrs. Jackson. She knows how to go about things and she can tell you what to do."

A short time later the housekeeper came into the room weeping. "Good heavens above us. It's a sad day to be sure, Miss Bevie. Was he struck down or did his heart give out?"

It was the first time Bevie had allowed herself to name the cause of his death. She stood up, shaking her head in horror. "Someone shot him. Who would have wanted to harm him? I cannot fathom it."

"Sit down, love. You have had a terrible shock. Go and bring up some strong tea, Suzie, while we discuss what is to be done."

Franklin remained in the library long enough to relate his version of events to Detective Oxenbrigg. "Oh, she done it alright. He must've bonked her on the head tryin' to stop her from pullin' the trigger. That there one's a spoilt one, I tell ye, wearin' them fancy gowns 'n all."

"Have you observed them in some previous altercation, Mr. Franklin?"

"Not seen 'em in a scuffle or nothin' if that's what yer after, but you can be sure she wants 'er way and gets it most of the time."

"How long have you been employed in the house, Mr. Franklin?"

"A right long time, Mr. Oxerpig."

"Oxenbrigg. How long?"

"Almost a year. It will be a year."

"When will it be a year?"

"In just about six months from now. I knowed him well, but she was uppity and spoilt I tell ye, Mr. Oxenpigger."

"Oxenbrigg. Thank you, Franklin. That will be all. Send in the housekeeper, if you please."

Mrs. Jackson was not only an efficient housekeeper, but she had become very fond of the family she served. Lord Burnside had been extremely good to her and she determined to do everything in her power to help his poor, grieving daughter.

"You must listen to me now, child. You hold your head high and never mind those rag-mannered fools. Never did I hear such nonsense. When they question you, as they will continue to do, you must say no more than what you have already told them, which is that you did not do it. Hear me now, Miss Bevie. I have known you since you were a babe and I will find someone to help you through this. Something smells very rotten in the whole affair."

There was a knock on the door and Mrs. Jackson was summoned to the library for questioning. However, Detective Oxenbrigg was not prepared for the tongue-lashing she proceeded to give him. Before he had finished his interrogation, he found himself gradually moving away from the woman and inching backward out of the library. He started to flee toward the front entrance and was met by Constable Green returning to the house.

"Just where do ye think you are going, man?"

"Er, I was, well – I think I have finished here."

"Just what makes your yellow-bellied self think ye are finished here?" snarled the constable.

Detective Oxenbrigg stood silently waiting for a further dressing down.

"You will take Lady Beverley to the constabulary for questioning."

"Indeed, sir. You won't be needin' that housekeeper, will you?"

"No, why?"

"Just wondered is all, sir."

Detective Oxenbrigg proceeded to inform Bevie of their required destination. It was not long before his greatest fear was realized when Mrs. Jackson declared that Bevie was going nowhere without a chaperone and that the chaperone would be none other than herself.

The two women were escorted into a sparsely furnished room containing a desk and several chairs. There were two windows in the room. One window looked outside to the city street and the other into the main part of the constabulary. Bevie sat in a chair and stared at the bare walls in a daze. Mrs. Jackson paced around the room, her countenance growing angrier by the minute.

She had just decided to storm out to the reception desk when, out of the corner of her eye, she caught a glimpse of a familiar face. She rapped on the window several times before she got the attention of her intended target.

The man, whose age was somewhere in his fourth decade, wore his years with ease and disregard. The lines around his keen brown eyes told of his frequent mirth. He was dressed in a top hat, a coat with long tails, and highly-polished buckle-shoes. He wore spectacles and carried a walking stick on which he was leaning at that particular moment.

He stroked his beard, sensing that he was being watched. He looked up and tipped his hat, surprised to see his friend. Mrs. Jackson motioned for him to come inside the room where they awaited interrogation. He rushed to enter the room and inquired as to the reason for her presence in such a place.

"My dear Mr. Hydemark, allow me to present Lady Beverley. It seems we are in the pickling barrel at the moment."

Bevie nodded politely. Mr. Hydemark bowed, swinging his hat widely to the side.

"May I ask what has transpired to plunge you into the pickling process, Mrs. Jackson?"

"Oh, it is not I, but my poor Lady Beverley who is being accused of a terrible crime. You may rest assured of her innocence, you see."

"Perhaps you will explain the situation to me," Mr. Hydemark suggested.

Their conversation was abruptly interrupted by the gruff Constable Green. "Hydemark, what are you doing in here? You have not been given leave to question this girl. Just because we use the information you give us now and then – though it seems of little use to me – does not permit you to run roughshod over the entire place."

"Forgive me, Constable Green, but I was just having a wee chat with my old friend, Mrs. Jackson."

"Then be off with you and visit her at another time and place."

Mr. Hydemark bowed to the ladies. "It will be my honor to attend you this evening, Mrs. Jackson. Thank you for the invitation," he said with a twinkle in his eye.

Mrs. Jackson understood perfectly that he intended to come to Burnside Court that very evening to inquire about the circumstances of the tragedy.

CHAPTER TWO

Cecil Busslingthorpe slapped the newspaper down on the table and took a sip of his tepid tea. The announcement of the death of his distant relative, Earl of Burnside, was of more than a little interest to him. He had spent a great deal of time and money – the latter of which he had almost none – tracing his family tree in order to establish his position in the succession of Burnside earls. Since the earl had no sons, it was unmistakable that he was the heir apparent as far as the title was concerned, but he had not been able to determine whether or not the estate was entailed and might lawfully come to him as well.

For nearly a year, he had courted the rather plain-looking Lady Mary, daughter of the wealthy Duke of Stokesbury. However, Stokesbury had forbidden their union on the basis that Busslingthorpe had no title and certainly no money.

Cecil had vaguely suggested to Mary that they elope, but she was devoted to her family and refused to bring such disgrace upon them. The event of the death of Burnside would strip away the duke's objection to his lack of a title and, with a bit of luck, he would inherit the estate as well. With Lady Mary's dowry added to the account, he would at last be well-situated.

He summed up his options and decided to wait another day before he approached Burnside's family to offer proper condolences. As he studied the newspaper article again, he learned that Burnside had one daughter who was apparently his only surviving immediate family member. He smiled as he realized how easy and uncomplicated it would make the transition since he would not be required to displace Burnside's widow when he took up residence in the elegant manor. As for the daughter – she would simply have to find her own way in the world just as he had done.

Cecil's mother, Araminta Busslingthorpe, had pushed him in the direction of Lady Mary in spite of the fact that she loathed the Duke of Stokesbury whom she had known when they were young. The duke had spurned her and, consequently, she decided she would have sweet revenge if her untitled and penniless son eloped with his only daughter. Unfortunately, the girl had more sense than Araminta imagined.

Having become excessively weary of living in distressed circumstances from long before the time of her no-good husband's death, Araminta set out to find possible relief in the form of some wealthy relative. She reasoned that being a poor relation was better than suffering through the cold winters without adequate heat. She vaguely remembered that her father had once mentioned a distant connection to the Earl of Burnside. She launched into a campaign to encourage her son to follow the family line and determine the exact relationship.

Once the discovery was made that her son was next in line for the title, her hopes soared and she began to devise a means of gaining the *haute ton's* attention to her dear Cecil's lofty position. She first attempted to extract invitations to social functions where she hoped to meet Burnside. She immediately received the royal cut from the very person in which she had placed her hopes and the connection never took place.

Now that the earl was dead, the fulfillment of Araminta's fondest dream was just over the horizon. She entered the breakfast room, surprised to see her son there.

"My dear boy, I did not know you had returned. I am so delighted to see you."

"And I you, Mother, but how did you sustain that nasty cut on your arm?"

"Oh it is nothing. I merely fell against a protruding nail in the upper hallway. We must move away from this crumbling pile, Cecil. Have you heard the news of Burnside's demise?"

"I was just now reading the account in the newspaper."

"Well, we have much work to do in that regard. Incidentally, where did you go when you left without so much as a by-your-leave?"

"I had some business with an old friend who lives near Wycombe."

"Did you indeed? Be that as it may, it is necessary that we find a way to be present at Burnside Court for the reading of the will, is it not?"

"I supposed that I would be summoned to attend since I am to inherit the title."

"Does the newspaper say when the funeral will take place? We should make haste and prepare to travel." Araminta's head was filled with scenes of great balls at Burnside Court where she would be the envy of all those of the *ton* who had snubbed her. Naturally, she would not include their names on the list of invited guests.

"Why are you smiling, Mum?"

"Oh, I was just thinking that you shall make a fine earl, my dear. You are so very poised and brave. You were born to the station."

"Yes, quite, although I haven't felt very much like Quality while we are forced to live in squalor."

"You exaggerate our circumstances, my dear, but we shall soon enjoy all of the privileges of the wealthy."

"I rather think it will take some practice to act accordingly. I haven't yet learned to stare coldly through my pince-nez in order to intimidate certain disagreeable persons and then completely ignore those beneath me, but I am quite good at the card tables."

"You will soon be able to do as you please. Imagine – my son, the Earl of Burnside. I am so happy I could cry."

"I think it best that you do cry frequently, Mother. The expectation is that we shall be dreadfully shocked and frightfully sad at the funeral."

"Yes, of course. You are very wise, milord," she quipped.

Constable Green had no mercy when he and one of his detectives questioned and attempted to intimidate Bevie into making a confession.

Mrs. Jackson sat close to her and whispered, "Remember what I told you, dear."

"I can only say that I found my father on the floor and I did not shoot him," Bevie said for the tenth time.

"I fear that is not good enough, miss. You are required to remain here until the coroner's report is delivered," Green proudly announced.

Bevie stared at the floor. It suddenly occurred to her that no one had mentioned a gun. "Have you found the weapon?"

"Aha," said Green. "Now we are getting closer to the truth. Where have you hidden the gun?"

"I don't have a gun," Bevie said calmly, "nor have I ever fired one. Let me go home. I do not believe you have enough evidence to keep me here."

"Of course we do. You were found lying next to the body. We have also found blood on the desk and on the wall near the door. What more evidence do I need?"

"You need to prove that I was not another victim of the attack."

Constable Green stammered and tried to contrive a proper response to her statement. He knew he could not keep her without more substantial evidence, but he was certain they would find it. "Very well, but I intend to station my deputy at your door to prevent your flight."

Bevie tried to hold her rage in check. "Shall I fly away to a sunny paradise while my father lay still in his coffin, Constable Green?"

Later that evening, Mr. Hydemark found Mrs. Jackson attending the distraught Lady Beverley in the drawing room where she had been sitting motionless for some hours, refusing to eat or be consoled. He was shown into the room by Franklin who would not look into the eyes of the girl he had accused of murder.

"Please forgive my intrusion into such a sad family matter, my dear ladies."

Mrs. Jackson stood to welcome her friend. "Do come in and sit with us, Mr. Hydemark. We are in a quandary as to what must be done."

"It is indeed a perplexing situation. There is little that can be done for your dear father, Lady Beverley, but there is much that can be done for you."

Bevie looked up through watery eyes. "I cannot see that anything can be done for me. I have lost my one and only family member and I have nowhere to turn."

"We may always turn to God, you see. He is the only one who sees the entire picture and He is the one who is our help in troubled times."

"If that is the case, then why did He allow a vicious murderer to take my father's life?"

"Ah, that is a secret He keeps from us until we meet Him face to face. I dare say your father now understands."

"How can you be sure?"

"I did not know your father, but I can only hope he had faith in Christ. Now, as to the practical side of things, perhaps you can explain the details of the tragedy to me."

Bevie told the sad story once again, trying to remember every detail.

"Are you certain your father was dead at the moment you arrived on the scene?"

"No, but when I recovered from the faint, I put my head on his chest and there was no heartbeat."

"How long would you say it was from the time you arrived until you opened your eyes to see Franklin standing over you?"

"I am not certain."

Mr. Hydemark continued to address both of them with many questions as to whom had arrived at the house that day, how many servants were on the staff, whether or not Lord Burnside had recently offended anyone, and so forth.

"Do you know the name of your father's man of law?"

"I have never met him, but I believe I have heard my father speak of a Mr. Desford in that regard."

"Has anyone from your household contacted him?"

"I don't know. I suppose I would be the likely person since Mr. Hughes, my father's accountant and man of business, has gone away to Spain to attend an ailing relative. Well, it may have been France. I am not certain."

"Perhaps you will allow me to take care of some of these details for you. It stands to reason that since you are a young woman and an only child, your father will have designated a protector for you in case of his early demise."

Just the mention of her father made Bevie begin to sob again.

Hydemark stood up. "I shall immediately work at putting together a defense for you. I am, you see, a solicitor by trade, but am currently in the business of snooping."

Mrs. Jackson quickly jumped in to explain to Bevie just what the man meant. "You see, my dear, Mr. Hydemark is the most remarkable detective that ever worked on the side of justice without actually being employed by Scotland Yard. Shall I ring for tea, Mr. Hydemark?"

"I do thank you, Mrs. Jackson, but I have many people to see yet this evening. If the invitation stands, I would be most grateful for a spot of tea two days hence."

"We shall look forward to it," replied Mrs. Jackson.

Mr. Hydemark took Bevie's hand and assured her that he would do all he could to help her. Mrs. Jackson accompanied him to the door while Bevie retired to her room.

In the stillness of the night, Bevie wondered if Mr. Hydemark could prevent her from being charged with murder. She decided he was simply blowing smoke and had no business interfering in her affairs. At that moment, she cared very little about her future. She fell asleep in her gown. Suzie removed her slippers and covered her with a counterpane.

Nearly every night when the house was finally locked up and quiet, Franklin, the butler, hurried to the corner of his room and knelt down beside a painted, wooden box that sat under an old wash tub. He slowly slid aside the false bottom and lovingly took out the strong box that had belonged to his father. He studied it for a moment before he opened the top and carefully counted the money, handling each coin with tender regard.

He smiled when he realized that his dream of a vacation on the Continent would soon be a reality. Mr. Hughes, Burnside's man of business, had told him of the pleasures and wonderful climate in both Spain and France. Visions of beautiful ladies dressed in vivid colors and a sandy beach beside a warm, blue ocean floated through his mind.

After all, he reasoned, it wasn't as if he had actually committed the offensive deeds himself. The guilty bloke simply handed him a few coins here and there in exchange for his silence concerning what he knew about Hughes and his friend altering the accounts of the estate.

Since Burnside was dead, Franklin saw a perfect opportunity to ask Hughes for much more than a mere trickling of coins. He had only to promise to keep his mouth shut if anyone questioned him about what he knew of the caper. Hughes had the nerve to tell Burnside he had been called to his aunt's home in Spain to help care for a dying uncle. In fact he was, at that moment, reclining on the beach and enjoying the warm breezes in the South of France.

Franklin began to imagine the events of the following days when he would have the opportunity to ask Hughes for more money. His only concern revolved around the question of when the renegade would decide to return to England. "He'd better do it soon else the whole thing'll come crashing down on his lyin', bald head," he mumbled.

His thoughts were interrupted by a light tapping on his door. He hurriedly closed the box and shoved it under the bed. "Who are ye and what do ye want at this time of night?"

"It is Mrs. Jackson."

"Go away, I want me sleep."

"Open the door or I'll break it down."

"Alright, hold on ta yer breeches, ye old bag."

He opened the door and tried to block her entrance, but Mrs. Jackson pushed her way into his room. She was surprised to see that he had kept it tidy since the last time she gave him a calling-down when the maid found a grand mess and complained about it. She took a few steps toward the bed. First, she caught sight of the wooden box in the corner with the lid standing open. Next, she spotted two coins on the floor next to the bed. She thought it odd, but decided not to mention it.

"I came to tell you that your presence will be required at the preliminary inquest tomorrow."

"Cor, why me?"

"The answer to your stupid question is simply that you happen to be the no-good butler who discovered the body and then proceeded to blame our dear Bevie for the murder. For all I know, you did it yourself and then tried to put the blame on her."

Franklin threateningly took a step toward her and growled. "Get out of here and stop flappin' yer lips, woman."

"A strange man ye are, Franklin." She turned and left the room.

Suzie was standing at the foot of the bed when Bevie opened her eyes the following morning. "There's a gentleman and his mother here to see you, miss. He says he is related."

Bevie sat up straight. "Did he give his name?"

"Yes, miss, but I am not sure – it was Brisslecone or something like that. Sorry, but I didn't understand him."

"It's quite alright, Suzie. It is very impolite for him to call at such an early hour. He may wait until I am ready to see him. I don't recall ever meeting any such relative."

"I hope he ain't one of them poor relations what lands on the doorstep as soon as they hear some mort with money passed."

"Whatever do you mean?"

"Never you mind, miss. Let me help you with your toilet. I'm trying to find your black gown. I think I seen it in the back of the wardrobe. You will have to see Madame Surrey today so she can make up some mourning clothes for you."

"I would not have thought of it, Suzie. I must try to think properly. I seem to be in a daze. Where is Mrs. Jackson?"

"She has to take care of the guests. She says to tell you not to hurry."

"Very good, I don't intend to do so."

Cecil and Araminta gladly accepted the invitation to sit at the breakfast table and partake of tea, coffee, fresh eggs, rashers of bacon, toast, and a variety of fruit. They had scarcely eaten on the journey and were famished, which was evident by the amount of food they consumed.

They had barely finished eating when Bevie entered the room. "Good morning. I believe I am at a great disadvantage, never having met either of you."

A very thin man of medium height with carrot-red hair, a very white complexion befitting the hair, small eyes, a pointed nose, and having the appearance of one of about thirty years, jumped out of his chair and bowed.

"How truly devastated we were to read of the sudden passing of our cousin, Thomas. I am Cecil Busslingthorpe and this is my mother, Mrs. Araminta Busslingthorpe. I sincerely regret that we have never had the pleasure of meeting you and terribly sorry that we were not able to know your dear, late father. I, naturally, have kept up with the grand things he accomplished over the years and am aware that he led a very fruitful life," Cecil blathered on, making it up as he went along.

Bevie brushed past him and sat down at the table. She hadn't eaten since the terrible event and was feeling faint. "How kind of you to come so *very early* in the day," she said sarcastically. "Since Mrs. Jackson has seen to your comfort, I know you will excuse me while I have my breakfast. Please feel free to wait in the drawing room and I shall endeavor to join you presently," she said quietly, obviously dismissing them.

"Of course, how kind of you," offered Araminta, entirely missing the intent of Bevie's words.

Cecil understood perfectly. He stood behind his mother and suddenly pulled her chair out from under her, nearly landing her on the floor. "Come, Mother, we must allow – say now, I don't believe you mentioned your name, miss."

"Lady Beverley."

"Yes, Lady Beverley, we shall await your presence in the drawing room."

Bevie alternated between anger and sadness. How dare they infringe on her breakfast, not to mention her private mourning.

Mrs. Jackson found her as she was finishing her toast. "There you are, dear. I suppose you've met those interlopers. My goodness, they haven't the manners of gutter rats. However, they do believe they are related to the earl, God rest his soul. In fact, Franklin told me he overheard the young man saying he meant to inherit the title of Sixth Earl of Burnside. Imagine anyone having the audacity to say such a thing."

Bevie took a sip of the strong coffee she had requested. "Perhaps it is true, Mrs. Jackson. Surely you know that, as a female, I cannot inherit the title. That puts me in mind of the fact that I must do something about the legal matters of the estate."

"You leave those worries to others, Miss Bevie. I received some correspondence from Mr. Hydemark this morning saying that he contacted your Mr. Desford who intends to call on you in a day or two. Now as to that business man, Hughes, I have my own thoughts, but Mr. Hydemark is kindly attempting to contact him as well."

Franklin entered the room and announced the arrival of Detective Oxenbrigg.

"Tell that tiresome man to wait in the sunroom where he will not come in contact with those other annoying visitors," Bevie ordered.

"But he . . ."

"Good morning, Lady Beverley," said the detective as he barged into the breakfast room.

"Doesn't anyone respect the fact that I require a little privacy at this hour of the morning, Detective Oxenbrigg?"

Oxenbrigg hung his head. "Sorry, but my orders were to deliver a summons to you." He handed her a folded paper. "I believe you will be required to attend the preliminary inquest this morning."

"Why should such a thing be required of me? It will be the end of me," Bevie moaned.

"My orders are to see that you appear, Lady Beverley."

"I shall, of course, accompany you, dear," announced Mrs. Jackson as she directed a scowl toward the detective.

"If you insist, ma'am, but my orders do not include you."

"Now isn't that just like a person of your questionable character. How dare you refuse to allow a chaperone to accompany an unmarried young lady of Quality. I suppose you have designs on her person," Mrs. Jackson accused, attempting to level him.

Detective Oxenbrigg's face beamed a bright red. "I will wait in the sunroom," he said, turning toward Franklin.

"I don't know how I shall manage to get through it, Mrs. Jackson."

"Nonsense, you will go about it with the courage I know you possess. Your father would have wanted you to be strong."

"Yes, I suppose he would have done so."

Bevie could not finish her breakfast. She reluctantly went to the drawing room to meet with her uninvited and unwanted guests. She entered the room and bluntly asked, "Will you require rooms for the night?"

Cecil stood and bowed. "Please sit down for a moment, Lady Beverley. I have something to tell you that might be of particular interest."

"Save it, Mr. Busslingthorpe. I have been advised that you believe you are the next Earl of Burnside. If that is true, let be what will be. Just now, I prefer to mourn in private. If you wish lodging here, I will inform the housekeeper."

"Yes, thank you, she has seen to our needs. We intend to stay until after the reading of the will."

Bevie nodded and turned to leave.

"One moment if you please, Lady Beverley, I do not wish to distress you further, but will you kindly tell me the name of your father's man-of-law and when he is expected to arrive?"

"I understand that Mr. Desford is expected to arrive in a day or two." With that, Bevie proceeded to deal with Oxenbrigg in the sunroom.

"It is not necessary for you to drag me kicking and screaming to the inquest, sir. Have no fear, Mrs. Jackson and I shall attend. Please leave my home – at least it is my home for the moment."

"But, I am only following orders, miss."

"Indeed, I am sorry for it, but Franklin feels compelled to assist you to the front entrance. Is that not true, Franklin?"

Franklin stood a foot above and a foot wider than the detective. When he began to move toward the detective, Oxenbrigg fairly ran out the door and stood with his horse at the edge of the carriage path where he was able to view the comings and goings of the household.

Madame Surrey, Bevie's French modiste, waited for her in her rooms. She had made gowns for Bevie on many occasions and brought with her four ready-made mourning dresses in black and varying shades of gray.

"Stand up long, miss," she ordered in her thick accent. "This one is too tall for you. I will get rid of that worthless seamstress. She always is making in the wrong size."

"I don't care. Just get me something to properly cover me. I am not concerned about fashionable dresses."

"Oh, but you must be always concerned about the fashion, my lady. It is always with importance, especially when you are sad."

Mrs. Jackson interrupted the session. "Mr. Hydemark has arrived. I have put him in the conservatory and the maids are preparing rooms for the guests."

"Thank you, Mrs. Jackson, I shall attend Mr. Hydemark presently. After that I would have a private word with you, please."

"Of course, simply ring when you require my presence."

Mr. Hydemark stood and approached Bevie as she entered the conservatory. They exchanged greetings and Mr. Hydemark led Bevie to a comfortable seat among the plants. He sat down opposite her where they could speak quietly.

"I have done some footwork concerning your situation, dear Lady Beverley. First of all, would you allow me to accompany you to the preliminary inquest today? I have had much experience in these things and perhaps I shall be able to deflect any ill-mannered scallywags from distressing you further."

"I would appreciate that, Mr. Hydemark. I do not believe I shall be able to bear it."

"Will you allow me to offer up a short request to our Lord?"

"Naturally, I will gladly take all the Divine help I can get."

"Lord, we are but mortals and lean upon Your all-powerful hand to deliver this child from those who would accuse her of this terrible deed. Comfort her and give her strength as we live each moment. In the name of Jesus Christ. Amen."

"Thank you Mr. Hydemark. Have you been able to contact Mr. Hughes, my father's man of business?"

"That is a cause for some concern. I have not been able to uncover the names of any of his relatives and none of his friends seem to know when he might return. I fear he may not return."

Bevie's mouth opened involuntarily and stayed in that position.

"Permit me to recommend that you seek the advice of Mr. Pick. He is my very good friend, and as it happens, he is an astute accountant. It would be wise to have him review the financial matters of the estate at once – that is, before the will is read. My reason for doing this is to avoid any havey-cavey nonsense should the estate be legally transferred to that young gentleman who is claiming that the title belongs to him."

"How did you know about him?"

"I have taken the liberty to know everything possible about the situation. If you object to my help, I shall indeed step aside and disappear from your presence."

"Please don't do that, Mr. Hydemark. I am extremely grateful for your help. I am lost, you see. I have no advisor and no one to make sure things are done properly."

"Yes, I am aware of your predicament. If you are willing to put yourself in my hands, I shall contact two of my acquaintances immediately. They are knowledgeable and capable of helping you with the details of the funeral and any other necessary arrangements."

"Yes, yes, I would like that above all."

"Good, then let us prepare for the preliminary inquest. Trust in the Lord to see you through this, Lady Beverley."

"I – I don't exactly know how to do that, sir."

"Have you confessed your sin to the Lord and believed that Christ is your Savior?"

"I have gone to church and learned the catechism."

"Then you know the facts. Now you must take them to heart and put them into practice."

CHAPTER THREE

William Henderson rolled out of bed at two in the afternoon. "Why are you bothering to awaken me at such an early hour, Carter?"

"News has come from Burnside Court that the earl is dead."

"What?"

"He was struck down yesterday. Lord Sedley requires you to be ready to call on the household in thirty minutes."

William groaned. "Send up my uncle's man to help me, Carter. My head is pounding."

"Very good, sir."

William grabbed a piece of meat from the sideboard as he hurried out the door to join his aunt and uncle who were waiting impatiently in the carriage. His mind had not yet clicked into gear when his uncle pointedly mentioned that Burnside had been shot.

William came to sudden attention. "What time did it happen?"

"That is exactly my question."

"You don't think that – no it couldn't have been…"

"How often have I warned you that your carelessness would lead to disaster one day?" Lord Sedley scolded.

"Whatever are you talking about, Bain?" Lady Sedley inquired.

"It is of no consequence, my dear."

William began to worry. "What shall we do, Uncle?"

"We will say and do nothing. Is that clear?"

"Yes, Uncle."

Their carriage turned onto the tree-lined lane at the same moment as the carriage with the Burnside crest flew past them in the opposite direction at a speed that was far too fast for the narrow carriage path. Sedley attempted to wave the driver to a stop, but the Burnside carriage was almost out of sight before his own came to a halt.

Believing that no one with any sense was riding inside the Burnside carriage, they continued on toward the house. William jumped out and ran to the front entrance in hopes of speaking with Bevie before other callers arrived. The under-butler opened the door and informed him that Lady Beverley was away from home.

"Invite me in, man. I shall await her return."

Not quite sure of the protocol in a house of mourning, the under-butler showed him in. He was led into the drawing room where an older woman dressed in black and a younger man wearing a black arm band sat idly. William bowed and introduced himself. Cecil stood and explained that he was a distant relative of the deceased.

A few minutes later, having determined that their nephew had been admitted, Lord and Lady Sedley joined the company. In the course of conversation, Lord Sedley learned that Bevie was under suspicion for the murder of her father and had been summoned to the preliminary inquest.

"Preposterous!" exclaimed Sedley.

Cecil stood and paced about the room with his hands clasped behind his back, choosing his words very carefully. "Perhaps it is, Lord Sedley. You see, I have no knowledge of the character of the young woman. She may possibly be given to bouts of temper. The butler, Franklin, seems to think she did it."

Cecil had taken some time to mull over the situation and decided that, if by some chance the estate was not entailed, it would be to his advantage to see little Miss Bevie behind bars or better yet, hung from the gallows. He pictured Lady Mary sitting at the head of the long dining table, smiling approvingly at him.

Sedley began to think he should say as little as possible. He wanted to keep William's name out of it at all cost. Perhaps if William's bullet was the one that killed Burnside and the police believed it had been Lady Beverley – well, he would simply have to wait and see what developed.

"It certainly is an extraordinarily dreadful event," Lord Sedley offered as a matter of conversation.

William's curiosity concerning Cecil was peaked. "Exactly how are you related to Burnside?"

Cecil held his head high and his long nose slightly tipped upward as he imagined an earl should do. "A cousin – distant, I suppose. However unfortunate the whole thing is, I am the new Earl of Burnside," he proudly announced before he realized he did not intend for the news to become known until the will was read.

The shock hit William like a pail of cold water. He wondered where that left Bevie as far as her dowry was concerned. *Surely the old man would have provided handsomely for her. I shall have to discover the exact arrangements before I do something so foolish as to marry a girl without a large dowry.* "Will you explain to us exactly why they believe Bevie would have done such a thing?" he asked.

"I am afraid we are not privy to the details," replied Cecil haughtily. "However, from what we can gather, Franklin found the girl lying next to the body and assumed Burnside had struck her in an attempt to keep her from shooting him."

Lady Sedley began to moan and sift through her reticule for her vial of vinaigrette. She let out a well-timed sob.

"There, there, my dear," said Sedley, patting her hand.

Bevie sat between Mrs. Jackson and Mr. Hydemark, leaning back on the leather squabs of the elaborately upholstered carriage. She glared at the fourth passenger who sat across from them, thinking she should push him out of the carriage and force him to walk to the inquest. Franklin smirked and pulled the curtain aside to look out at the passing scenery.

"How long do these dreadful inquests last?" she dared to ask Mr. Hydemark.

"It depends upon how complicated the case becomes. In this particular situation, I am afraid it is going take longer than we would wish. However, this is said to be a preliminary inquest which, in my short history, I find altogether unlawful and unnecessary."

Bevie wanted to be courageous and poised. She wanted to walk into the room with quick steps and a demure expression. But, when Mr. Hydemark opened the door to allow her to enter, she felt faint and almost wept.

Mrs. Jackson knew her very well and saw her fading. She took hold of her arm and led her inside, lifting up on her arm to force her to stand straight. "Lift your head and look straight ahead," she whispered in Bevie's ear.

It was expected that Bevie would be escorted to the front of the room where the suspects were normally seated, but instead, Mr. Hydemark hurried to guide her into a rear seat. Once again she sat between Hydemark and Mrs. Jackson. Franklin, however, sauntered to the front of the room, slowly and determinedly turned, looked around at the gathering, and then sat down on a bench in the first row.

The coroner stood up and raised his hand for silence. "Due to the fact that this is not an official inquest, the Officer of the Queen's Household is not in attendance and we shall dispense with the formalities."

Mr. Hydemark was on his feet before the man finished his sentence. "This is highly irregular, sir, and I must contend that it is not legal."

The audience disagreed with him and let it be known by their shouts of disapproval.

"I know who you are, Hydemark," said the coroner, "and you have no authority here. Sit down."

The coroner continued to announce full name of the deceased, date and place of birth, and date of death. "On the aforementioned date, I was called into service to determine the exact cause of death of the deceased. Due to the unusual circumstances, I have obtained the expertise of three well-qualified surgeons in order to secure their opinions on the matter. Let me say at the outset that, while our findings are unusual, it is never impossible to discover the primary cause of death and, thereby, the murderer."

Bevie was becoming more and more annoyed. "What is he talking about, Mr. Hydemark?"

"Shh, I suppose he will enlighten us before the day has ended."

The coroner continued, "Although my consultants differ somewhat in their findings, it has been discovered that one bullet entered the heart of the deceased from the back, another entered his brain from the front, and to further complicate matters, he had ingested a small amount of poison. A cup of liquid was spilled on the rug next to the victim making it impossible to determine whether or not it was the source of poison."

The chatter from the audience increased in volume until the coroner banged on the table at the front of the room where several men sat smoking and spitting in the spittoons that lined the sides of the table. The law-writer sat next to Constable Green trying to determine which words were worthy of record.

"Furthermore, Scotland Yard has determined that each bullet was fired from a different gun, making it difficult to determine whether one of the bullets or the poison was the cause of death and how many people were involved in the hideous crime." He went on to explain the types of guns that might have fired the bullets.

The audience became unruly, standing and shouting and demanding to know the names of the owners of the weapons.

"No weapons have been located at this time and Scotland Yard refuses to arrest any suspects."

Franklin was outraged. He stood and pointed directly at Bevie. "I found her slumped over the body. He tried to stop her but she shot him anyway. She done it, I tell you."

"Take your seat and be silent, man. Scotland Yard will do their job and, if what you say is true, she will be duly punished. Now, I am asking for testimony concerning the types of guns from which the shots came. If you have any knowledge of a person or persons owning one of these, we will hear your testimony now."

Several people stood and told of this person and that who might have had one such weapon at some time or another, but not one of them had anything worthwhile to offer as evidence.

At last, the coroner called the session to an end and the people filed out, never failing to glare directly at Bevie as they passed her.

She stumbled into the carriage and collapsed onto the seat. "It was worse than I expected," she whispered.

Franklin stood behind Mr. Hydemark waiting to enter the carriage for the ride home.

"Get that man out of my sight," Bevie nearly shouted. "I never want to see him again."

Mr. Hydemark turned and said something to Franklin that Bevie could not hear and then climbed in and sat next to her, tapped on the roof with his stick. The carriage moved forward, leaving Franklin behind.

"You must allow the man to collect his belongings if you have a notion to dismiss him, Lady Beverley," he explained. "Actually, I have reason to believe it would be to our advantage were you to keep him employed. In that way, we may discover the reason he is so determined to point the finger of guilt at you."

"What possible reason would he have to accuse me?"

"In my experience, I have found that most of the evil in the world points to the love of money, the quest for power, or occasionally, the desire to secure someone in a love match."

"I do not see how his presence can be of any use to me. I loathe the man."

"Perhaps in time God will help you to forgive him. However, I do not believe he is acting alone. There is something very significant in the way he ruthlessly accuses you of the crime in light of the fact that you are now his employer."

"I suppose that will change as soon as the will is read and that awful Busslingthorpe person casts me out of my home into the street."

"Perhaps he will not be so cruel."

Mrs. Jackson chimed in. "Surely your father will have provided a place for you to live."

"He did not expect to be murdered and leave me alone. He was not very old, you see." Bevie began to weep again just as the coachman reined in the horses in front of the house.

Mr. Hydemark accompanied the ladies up the steps. The under-butler opened the door and bowed. Before he could assist Bevie in removing her pelisse,

William came bursting into the hallway and took over the chore.

"Oh, Bevie, I am so very sorry to hear about your father. I suppose everything was settled at the hearing."

Bevie sniffled. "They still think I did it."

"Well, stap me. I can't believe it. By the by, I know of a cove up in Oxford who may take you on. He's thought to be a fine solicitor."

"Thank you, William, but I have not yet decided what I am to do."

Mr. Hydemark interrupted. "Good day, sir, I am Hydemark and might say that help is on the way for Lady Beverley."

Just as William opened his mouth to protest, the under-butler opened the door once again and announced the arrival of Mr. Frederick Styles, a noted solicitor, and Mrs. Mina Metterson, a lady of many virtues. Mr. Hydemark was obliged to make his friends known to the others, including William.

Introductions being made, Mrs. Jackson returned to her duties and Mr. Hydemark pointedly excused himself. "Lady Beverley and I must be allowed to speak privately with my friends as we have many things to discuss. I am certain you must understand."

"Ho now, Bevie, I am here to help you in any way I can. Say that I may be able to call on you this evening," begged William.

"Perhaps tomorrow, William. I cannot think straight at present."

"Your servant," he said, bowing and then hurrying away to collect his aunt and uncle.

Just after Sedley's carriage disappeared from view, a footman arrived with a note for Bevie. Franklin had resumed his position as butler and was tempted to open the correspondence, but the seal was unmistakably well-secured and he did not dare. He listened intently at the library door, hoping to hear what was transpiring. To his dismay, the people were speaking quietly and he could not make out more than one or two words. He knocked lightly on the intricately-carved oak door.

Mrs. Metterson opened the door and looked at him questioningly. He bowed appropriately and held out a silver tray bearing an envelope with Bevie's name printed on the front. Mrs. Metterson thanked him and closed the door. Franklin remained by the door, hoping to catch a phrase or two.

After a few moments of silence, Mrs. Metterson flung open the door frightening Franklin into a stupid-looking, opened-mouth expression.

"There is to be no reply, Franklin. Return to your duties and stop eavesdropping. If it were my home, you would be struggling to pick up your belongings from the stables and wearing a shoe mark on your sore backside."

Mrs. Metterson handed the note to Bevie.

"It is from father's man-of-law who informs us that he has been unavoidably detained for several days."

Mr. Styles spoke up. "That will work to our advantage, Lady Beverley, since the will cannot be read until he arrives. We need time to put our plans into action."

"Do you think there is a chance I will not be hung?"

Mr. Hydemark moved to the settee where Bevie sat and patted her hand. "We have every hope of finding the person who did this terrible thing. If you will allow Mr. Styles to act as your solicitor, I am sure you have no reason to worry."

Bevie turned to Mr. Styles. "I would be grateful if you would do so."

"I must make it clear that I have not had much experience in these matters, having only begun my solo work a few years ago. However, I have been trained by the masters of the craft and I will try my utmost to clear your name."

Bevie nodded. She began to have a flicker of hope for a moment and then immediately slipped back into a state of despair.

Mrs. Metterson prodded her for information regarding her father and his family, the latter of which seemed to be non-existent except for the intruders who had arrived on the scene shortly after the news of Burnside's death was published. She left the room with quick, light steps and began to make arrangements for the funeral.

Mrs. Metterson was an attractive widow of somewhere in the vicinity of thirty-five years. Her hair was pulled back tightly into a bun and she wore severely-cut, drab-colored dresses which tended to give her a stern demeanor. She never turned down an opportunity to arrange other people's lives, considering it had been her livelihood until she joined the Hydemark Agency. Her amazing ability to make things run without a snag or hitch had kept her in comfortable circumstances after her husband died. She was adept at launching young debutantes into society or planning elaborate balls and weddings for the *bon ton* who were not able, or did not choose to do so themselves.

On the way to success, however, she had ruffled a great many feathers. She was forthright, demanding, and for the most part, unsympathetic. She accepted no refusals, allowed for no tardiness, and expected complete conformity to each and every one of her demands.

On this occasion, she began to set things in motion for the timely funeral of Lord Burnside and the elaborate refreshments following the service. The first obstacle in her systematic preparation was that of the local vicar who had informed her that he would be unavailable for the entire week in which the funeral would occur.

The vicar stood at a distance as she spoke to him. "The inquest will be over in three or four days at which time the burial must take place immediately due to the time it has taken that lazy coroner to complete his investigation. Surely you must have suffered some terrible debilitation which has made it impossible for you to officiate at Lord Burnside's funeral. Dear me, can it be that you are dreadfully ill?"

"Well, no, but I have a previous engagement, you see."

"Let me ask you this, sir. Did Lord Burnside ever fail to pay his tithes or willingly meet your demands for extra funds and gifts of charity?"

"He did that, but as I said . . . "

"Is this the thanks he gets from you? Must the residents of Burnside Court transfer their allegiance to another parish in the future? I am shocked that you have not been at Lady Beverley's side from the moment the news of her father's murder fell on your ears. Never mind, Mr. Simple, I shall contact the bishop. I feel very certain that he will see things differently."

"Oh, please allow me to explain. I would normally . . ."

"Franklin, see Mr. Simple to the door," Mrs. Metterson said, turning away and walking quickly down the hallway. Little did Mr. Simple know that the bishop was her cousin.

When Bevie's head began to nod, Mr. Hydemark suggested she retire until the dinner hour. Mr. Styles assured her he would attend the official inquest and take care of any legal matters which concerned a trial that might follow.

Bevie's experience with the outside world was limited to a year in a Swiss finishing school that was located some distance from any sizeable city and was mostly isolated from society in general. Although she observed many of her classmates experiencing various hardships during the year, her life had run smoothly and without complications.

She was having difficulty understanding how anything so horrible as the present circumstance could happen to her and had no idea how to function under such terrifying threats. At times, she wondered if it would be easier to make a false confession and allow the powers that be to end her life sooner rather than later.

The next person to arrive at Burnside Court was an accountant who had been secured by Mr. Hydemark. Mrs. Jackson showed him to the library and unlocked the desk where Lord Burnside kept his financial records.

"Thank you, Mrs. Jackson, I wish to begin work immediately," he announced forthwith.

"I shall have a room prepared and have another place set at the table for you, Mr. Pick."

"Thank you, but I would prefer to have a dinner tray brought to me in here tonight. It is apparent that time is of the essence. Where might I find the secondary books kept by Mr. Hughes?"

"I will inquire of the staff, but unless I miss my guess Mr. Hughes has taken them away or destroyed them."

"Am I to understand that you believe he was not an honest man?"

"It is not for me to say, but I will be extremely relieved if you find the accounts in order."

"Where can the man be found? Does he live on the estate?"

"He has a cottage along the north edge of the estate. Only last month he asked permission of Lord Burnside to have leave to attend a dying uncle in Spain. To the best of my knowledge, he has not returned or corresponded with anyone here since that time."

"I see," Mr. Pick said, stroking his chin where he had recently removed a beard. "Kindly ask Hydemark to step in here. I would have a word with him."

"Certainly," Mrs. Jackson replied as she hurried from the room.

CHAPTER FOUR

William Henderson paced the floor in front of his uncle's desk. "You have friends in high places, Uncle. Would it not be possible for one of them to secretly uncover the contents of Burnside's will before it is read?"

"That would require a dishonest man of law and a professional fool, would it not? What sort of people do you think I associate with, William?"

"I think you do very well, but I am at a loss to know whether or not I should pursue an alliance with Bevie at this time."

"If that is the case, then perhaps you should not pursue her at all. She is a lovely girl, that is, aside from being overindulged by her father from the day of her birth. Return to your studies, William. You need the polish and could use some sharpening of your reasoning powers."

William excused himself and decided to call on Bevie. He had to do something soon if he wanted to avoid telling his uncle that his enrollment at Oxford would soon be terminated. He decided to chance courting Bevie on the basis of his expectation that Burnside would provide a respectable dowry and disposable funds for his only child. He thought he knew Burnside well enough to believe the man had enough regard for her to do so.

He shuddered at the memories of their childhood when Bevie easily bested him in almost every contest or race they entered. As he pondered the solution to his problem, he decided to forgive her for those maddening assaults on his manhood, particularly since she was undoubtedly blessed with a handsome dowry which would serve to carry him nicely along until he inherited from his uncle – and possibly far beyond.

She had never shown any romantic interest in him, but he felt certain he could slowly change her mind. "After all," he reasoned aloud, "I am the sort of dandy most girls seek to drag before the parson."

He searched his wardrobe for some clothing that he imagined would make him look sleek, slightly rugged, and more athletic than his ever-thickening middle section normally indicated. Having no servant, he attempted to comb his hair in a style that befitted a Corinthian. He left word with Carter that he would not return for the evening meal and turned his horse in the direction of Burnside Court.

Henry Pick poured over Burnside's books with total concentration. Mr. Hydemark stood quietly by waiting for him to look up, which he did not.

"You have a most intense expression, Henry. Have you found something unusual?"

"Not exactly, although I have an unsettled feeling that something is not right. It is all too perfect. I have two questions for you, Hydemark. Are we able to break into Hughes' cottage and . . . are you on friendly terms with any of the upper management of the Front Street Bank?"

"Perhaps and yes."

"Then let us be about the first item. The other will wait until business hours on the morrow."

"We have two or three days until the funeral, Henry. Is it possible for you to wrap this up before the reading of the will, which I assume will take place directly following the funeral?"

"That, my friend, will depend on how adept you are at breaking and entering, as well as how intimately you are acquainted with the top men at the bank."

"Let us be off, then."

"Oh, there is one more thing, Hydemark. I have noticed a mysterious-looking strongbox box on the top shelf over there," he said pointing upward. "Is there a chance we might find a key and have a look inside?"

"Most assuredly, but first let us take a short walk to Hughes' cottage."

They strode away from the mansion, acting as though they were merely exercising after hours of sedentary work. Mr. Hydemark's pockets were filled with various tools of his trade.

When they arrived at the cottage, they knocked to make certain it was not occupied. They separated and walked in opposite directions around the dwelling in order to survey the area for possible onlookers, eventually meeting at the back of the cottage. Mr. Hydemark took out his remarkable tool that sprung the lock on the back door with ease.

They went over the premises with a fine-tooth comb, so to speak. They had all but given up finding anything useful when Mr. Pick spoke up.

"Here, Hydemark, have a look at this little book of accounts. I found it in the cushion of this chair as though it had been lost."

"Well, well, let us check the handwriting against the books at the court, but I would almost swear it is the same hand as our Mr. Hughes. It seems as if our friend has been keeping track of some sort of payments he's been receiving. The entries are so varied that we must suppose they were not his salary and that someone was paying him for something else."

They took one more pass over the cottage and returned to the mansion, only to be disappointed when they discovered the handwriting did not match that of Hughes.

Mrs. Metterson asked Bevie to meet her in the sunroom. She was tired and needed to rest from her labors for a few minutes. Bevie was surprised to see her sitting with her feet propped up and her shoes on the floor beside her.

"Come and have a seat beside me, dear girl. What a dreadful time it is for you. I wanted to review the arrangements for the funeral with you before I finalize the plans."

"It is very kind of you to help, Mrs. Metterson, but I cannot care what the arrangements are – only that they will honor the memory of my father. I have no interest in the people who will attend or anything else, for that matter. I only wish to be left alone."

"I know how you must feel, Lady Beverley, but allow me to remind you of your obligation to uphold your father's name and position. It is one of the many times in life that one must become a superb actress. When things are at rock bottom, we must hold our heads up and smile graciously at those who show an interest in our welfare. It is expected of the *ton*, you see."

"And what should I care of the *ton*? They have not shown any interest in me except to gossip, and I sincerely hope they will not begin to pretend they care at this time."

"I see. Well, let me suggest that if you sulk in a corner and hide from people, the dreadful accusations that have produced a great deal of gossip about you will seem to be true. I must advise you to purposely set your demeanor to reflect your innocence in the matter. Let us give no cause for the *ton* to take sides against you. There are a great many powerful people among them."

"What good is it if I should act as though I shall escape the gallows?" Bevie began to cry.

Mrs. Metterson moved behind Bevie's chair and put her hands on her shoulders. "You have no idea what the peers of the realm can accomplish, Lady Beverley. Why, even if you were guilty, they could defend you with such skill that everyone would believe in your innocence. Many criminals have gone free because of them. In addition to that, you have Mr. Hydemark. He is the most remarkable man I know. He can coax a mouse out of its hole without the aide of cheese. You must have faith in him."

"Interesting you should say that. He told me to have faith in God – not him."

"Yes, that is certainly true, but have you not heard that God works in mysterious ways? I believe He uses Mr. Hydemark as one of those mysterious ways."

Bevie sat quietly contemplating what Mrs. Metterson had said. The thought crossed her mind that had her mother lived, she might have given the same advice.

"Thank you for helping me, Mrs. Metterson. I feel as though you have given me some things to think about. I appreciate your candor. I count you as my friend and wish you would call me Bevie."

"Thank you, dear."

Franklin came striding boldly into the sunroom without knocking. Mrs. Metterson began to reprimand him, but let her words die in midair and decided to allow the incident to slide.

"A gentleman has called for Lady Beverley. It is William Henderson."

Bevie groaned. "Tell him I will join him shortly, Franklin," Bevie said quite civilly to the butler who had accused her.

After Franklin left the room she spoke to Mrs. Metterson. "There, how was that for someone who wishes to string the butler up by his toes?"

"You did very well, Bevie. Remember, I shall be at your side whenever you need me."

Bevie thanked her and reluctantly walked toward the drawing room. She dreaded seeing William.

Henry Pick paced in front of the tall glass doors of the library that led to the terrace. He walked to the desk, smacked a sheaf of papers on the edge of it, turned, and walked back to the double doors. He decided to talk with every hired person inside Burnside Court. He paced in front of the doors again, observing the gathering clouds, and then stopped in his tracks. He put his finger through the bullet hole in the door, wondering how he could have missed seeing it. He rang for Mrs. Jackson.

She came breathlessly into the room. "This place is going to be the end of me," she sighed. "What can I do for you, Mr. Pick?"

"I am sorry to add to your duties, Mrs. Jackson, and I would not do so if I did not think it crucial. Will you be kind enough to arrange an interview with every one of the hired help? I shall begin the task in one hour and will only require each one to be present for five or ten minutes. It would be particularly helpful if they would assemble in groups of ten and queue outside this room."

"That is a very difficult task at this time of day, Mr. Pick, as they are all very busy preparing for the evening meal."

"I am very sorry, Mrs. Jackson, but there is a life at stake. Do you know where I might find Hydemark at this hour?"

As if carried there by angels, Mr. Hydemark appeared in the doorway.

"Come with me to the conservatory, William. I simply cannot stand this dreary room," Bevie said, motioning for William to follow her. She felt quite comfortable with him since they had been childhood playmates, but she had never thought of him as anything other than a neighbor and did not have the slightest romantic interest in him.

"At your service, my lady," he said with an exaggerated bow. He, unlike Bevie, was thinking very seriously along the lines of romance, or at least some sort of courtship that would lead to marriage – and securing her dowry. If circumstances had been different and his uncle had deeper pockets, he would never consider becoming leg-shackled at this time in his life. He loved the fast-paced life and all the entertainments he enjoyed with his friends at Oxford. He loathed the idea of giving it all up.

As the two ambled down the hallway, Mrs. Jackson came out of the library leaving the door ajar, greeted the pair briefly, and went off in the opposite direction. William slowed his steps and peered into the room. At that moment, Henry Pick was showing Mr. Hydemark the bullet hole in the glass door.

William stopped short. He heard Mr. Hydemark suggest that the bullet that had passed through the door may have been the one that killed Lord Burnside. His heart began to beat so rapidly that he could hardly breathe.

"Come along, William. Why are you stopping here?"

"I was – am just – oh, forgive me, Bevie. I was thinking that I must – it seems I have forgotten an important engagement with someone who's come down to the city from Oxford."

Bevie started to tell him that he should not keep the fellow waiting, but her words were cut short by a rather loud commotion at the front of the house. They hurried to see what was happening and arrived just in time to see someone pushing Franklin aside.

Franklin was shouting indignantly at the person. "Hold up before I stop you dead in your tracks!"

The young woman ignored him and pressed forward.

"Oh my darling girl," said the familiar voice, "I came as soon as I heard. How extremely unfortunate this is for you. Who is that odious man tending your front door? He keeps shouting at me. I should think he is useless as a doorman."

"Petra? How did you know?" cried Bevie, running into the arms of the person who had been her constant companion at the finishing school in Switzerland.

The two girls embraced as William stood back wondering about the identity of the tall, attractive, dark-haired stranger. He cleared his throat, hoping to call attention to his presence.

"Oh, forgive me, William. This is my dear friend Petra Gabrieli who has come all the way from . . .where did you come from, Pet?"

"It doesn't matter, darling. I am here to bear you up in your time of grief." Petra turned to William and looked him over brazenly. "Who exactly might you be, sir?"

Before William could answer, Bevie spoke up, "He is my neighbor. We have known each other since William was in short coats. He was just leaving for an engagement with his friend."

William, still in shock from the scene he observed in the library, quickly excused himself and left.

"Is he a particular friend, Bevie? Does he have money or a title or some kind of fame? He does not seem to be your type of man."

"He is a pest. Never mind William. How did you come to find out about this horrible situation? Come and let me ask my housekeeper to prepare a room for you."

"No love, I would not dream of intruding upon your household. The fact is that I came to England only yesterday to visit with my brother in his newly purchased London townhome. He remembered your name, the dear boy, and put me onto the article in the newspaper. I could not believe it. How are you, darling? Can you possibly stand it?"

"I haven't been doing very well, but you are a ray of sunlight in the midst of a very black nightmare."

"Call for tea, love, and tell me about it from the beginning."

The outgoing and competent Petra sat quietly while Bevie related the entire tragedy. "This is a most dreadful situation, Bevie. Have you any idea who would commit such a crime?"

"I have tired my brain trying to imagine why anyone would do this.   My father and I were not extremely close, but he was a kind man and treated me very well.   I believe he missed my mother and, consequently, kept to himself a bit. He was somewhat private concerning his social life. He attended his club regularly two nights each week. He never discussed his friends or business with me, but he was always available when I needed him."

"Did he entertain?"

"Yes, I acted as his hostess on several occasions, but lately he had become more withdrawn from society."

"You are very fortunate to have had such a good parent, Bevie. Although my parents pretend to love me, they have never been around when I needed them. They have traveled over the earth with their beloved music and performed in nearly every country one can name. In the meantime, they moved me from place to place and school to school. You saw how it was in Switzerland. They visited me for one day and then they got restless and had to move on."

"I always believed that you led a glamorous life. By the bye, what happened to that handsome young man who was forever hoping to meet you secretly?"

"You speak of Pierre Renault," Petra said, looking down and seeming distraught as she spoke quietly in her delightful continental accent. "I nearly married him, Bevie."

"What happened?"

"I can hardly speak of it. We were so happy – at any rate, I believed we were. One day he took me to visit his family who live just outside Paris. I knew it would be only a matter of a few more days until he proposed marriage and I was up in the clouds. He had not told me that his family was very wealthy and I was stunned to find that they lived in what I would call a palace. Well, then the inevitable happened. His mother discovered that my parents were traveling musicians and she immediately put an end to our courtship. She held the strings to the family fortunes, you see."

"Yes, I do see. It seems that most men are more concerned about obtaining wealth than anything else."

"Yes, and I have come to believe that we should return the favor and have the same goals as they. I suppose many enlightened women do so."

Bevie thought about Mr. Hydemark. He did not seem to be interested in accumulating wealth. At that moment, she realized that she was the one who should be taking care of the household staff and paying out salaries as well as remunerating Mr. Hydemark and Mrs. Metterson for their constant diligence.

"What a slag I've been, Pet. You have just awakened me from a stupor. I have left everything at Burnside Court to rot away."

"It is only to be expected, darling. I am here to give you a push back into life just as you did for me when my younger brother died suddenly."

"Have you recovered from that terrible event, Pet?"

"I shall never completely recover, but time does make it more bearable. Now, let us return to your situation. Who is this man at the entrance who dares to accuse you and why do you keep him?"

"Franklin has been employed only for about six months, but Mr. Hydemark believes that we should keep him here so that we may watch him closely."

"Mr. Hydemark must be a remarkable man. However, I believe your butler needs to be taught some rules of etiquette."

William spurred his horse on toward home. He tethered it on the side of the house and crept into the hallway adjacent to the kitchen. His shoes were making noise on the wooden floor, requiring him to remove them before he reached the hallway next to the room where his uncle kept his guns. He searched the drawers in the chest until he found the key to the gun cabinet and took out the fine-looking rifle he had used in their recent hunting excursion. He carried it outside, carefully removed it from its leather case, and wrapped it in his hunting coat. His horse began foaming and he decided to take it to the stables and ask the one remaining stable boy to care for it. He took another animal to his next destination, thinking it would be a very good idea if his own horse were not seen going back toward Burnside Court.

Having carefully contrived the steps of his deceit, he took the gun to the gardener's shed on the Burnside estate. After searching for the best place, he removed the gun from its covering and hid it beneath one layer of mulch that he knew would be used by the gardener within a few days. He quietly rode away through the wooded path that led to his uncle's house.

Franklin was sitting on a bench outside the kitchen. He was puffing on a cigar which he had stolen from the library. He watched the whole incident with curiosity. After William was out of sight, he went into the shed and searched for the gun. He located it within three minutes.

"I won't be responsible if you fall from that ladder, Henry."

"I've got hold of the thing. Come here and take it from me."

Mr. Hydemark reached up and took the metal box.

"Lock the door, Hadley. I believe the servants are beginning to queue in the corridor for their interviews."

Mr. Hydemark unlocked the box with his trusty tool. Inside were loose papers. The two men hurried to examine them. "Gambling debts all," said Hydemark.

"And all from the same source – Sir Colin Darley," added Henry.

"Apparently all neatly paid off by Lord Burnside."

The two men stood silently for a moment before Hydemark spoke again. "I believe we have another suspect in the murder, Henry."

"How in blazes can that help us? What we have is three attempts at murder and we do not know which one of them actually killed the man."

"But who is the third suspect? Surely you cannot think his own daughter killed him."

"Probably not, but then it surely has happened before. I haven't had a chance to speak with her since we met briefly in the entry hall."

"Perhaps you should make it a point to know her better, Henry. I think you will agree with me that she is incapable of such a thing."

"All in good time, my fine friend. Just now I must interview a trainload of people. However, before I do so, I'm going outside to examine the area around the terrace for footprints. Kindly keep the crowd at bay until I return."

Hydemark sank into a chair and nodded. He was too tired to go with Henry.

Henry moved carefully down the long terrace, stepped onto the flower bed and made his way along the wall, passing the windows of the sunroom where Bevie and Petra sat with their empty tea cups.

Petra suddenly looked up. "Who is that gorgeous creature walking past the window?"

"Oh, it is only the accountant who is a friend of Mr. Hydemark – a Mr. Hick, I think."

"Never let him leave your sight, Bev. He is 'positively beautiful'."

"After what you have suffered at the hands of a 'positively beautiful' man, I believe I will allow this opportunity to pass."

"So wise. . . so very, very wise."

"Please say you will stay here with me, Pet." Bevie leaned toward her and whispered, "Father installed three more water closets and heated water baths before his death. Can you imagine it?"

"That is wonderful, darling, and I would love to stay. However, I have promised to act as hostess for a small entertainment my brother is planning for tonight. I regret that I must soon leave in order to check on the preparations."

"I have never met your brother, Pet. Is he older than you?"

"Nicolo is four and twenty. He is three years older and he is much more acquainted with the world than am I. My parents did not see fit to lock him up in dreadful boarding schools his entire life as they did to me."

"Do not become bitter, Pet. I believe they did what they thought was best for you."

"Perhaps, but let us speak of your future. I know you cannot go anywhere until this dreadful affair is settled. However, you must listen closely to what I am saying. If things do not go well for you in the courts, you must allow Nicolo to help you. He will spirit you out of the country before anyone knows of it. Nicolo has many friends and he has accumulated some wealth of his own. Also, I believe he is a wonderful and trustworthy person."

"I am so happy you have a good brother, Pet, but I cannot run away from my problems."

"We shall see. I must go now, darling."

Pet kissed her friend on both cheeks in the continental style. When she reached the entrance, she stopped in front of the rather large Franklin. "Hurry with my wrap, little man," she said as she reached up and patted him on the head.

Franklin developed splotches of red on his neck. He wished to throttle the girl.

Bevie did not move from the settee. She continued to contemplate her conversation with Pet. How she admired her friend's independence. But then, she wondered how Pet would have reacted were she caught in a similar situation.

Bevie also wondered if perhaps Pet was a bit too worldly. She studied the contrast between Mr. Hydemark and Pet. It seemed they were worlds apart, but she was unable to put her finger on the exact reason. Franklin came into the room and announced the arrival of Constable Green, jolting her back into the reality of her pressing problems.

CHAPTER FIVE

Cecil Busslingthorpe stood at the window observing Franklin hurrying from the garden shed into the house. He was carrying an object that looked altogether like a rifle. Cecil moved to the side of the doorway where he would be hidden from view. He hoped to discover the butler's destination. Franklin moved quickly toward the stairs. Cecil followed at a safe distance and observed him entering Lady Beverley's sitting area.

"What a clever idea," Cecil said to himself, "but one can only wonder what his reasons are for wanting her hung from the gallows."

Cecil ducked behind the statue in the hallway as Franklin passed by and returned to his duties. He wondered how long it would take for someone to find the weapon. His patience regarding his marriage to Lady Mary Stokes was wearing thin. He saw this as a possible chance to implicate Bevie in the murder, whereby he would inherit the Burnside estate and ingratiate himself to Mary's father. He toyed with the idea of alerting the law to the presence of the weapon.

However, he did not have long to wait for results. An hour later, Franklin attended the front door and admitted Constable Green and three uniformed police officers. Constable Green announced that a detailed search of the house would be underway presently.

Bevie, standing at the top the steps, heard the declaration and went directly to find Mr. Hydemark. She found him standing outside the library with a few of the kitchen staff.

"Please explain to me why members of the kitchen staff are standing idly around while they have duties to perform," she demanded.

"Have patience, my dear girl," begged Mr. Hydemark. Mr. Pick had the idea that he should briefly interview each person with regard to their duties and pay. Tomorrow is quarter day when they regularly receive compensation, is it not?"

"Yes, of course. I realize I have been remiss and should have taken over my father's duties until it is decided whether or not I will leave Burnside Court for good."

"Why not allow Pick to handle things in the interim, Lady Beverley? He is most adept at running things without a hitch."

"Yes, I would appreciate that. Did you know that Constable Green is on the verge of conducting a thorough search of the house?"

"No, is he? In that case, please excuse me while I notify Pick," he said, bowing to her.

Hydemark entered the library unannounced and closed the door leaving the few remaining servants waiting in the hallway. He informed Pick of the search and quickly stuffed the papers from the strongbox into his pocket. He wished to have a word with Colin Darley before the constable got wind of the gambling debt.

Cecil returned to the drawing room where he and his mother had situated themselves since their arrival. Araminta stood by the window wringing her hands.

"What is the matter, Mother?"

"Those men have asked me some very pointed questions. Why would they desire to question me?"

"Perhaps they need to gather some pertinent information about conversations you may have overheard in the household."

"Yes, that must be it. Thank you, dear. That relieves my distress."

Bevie walked down the path to the stables in order to avoid the detectives while they wreaked havoc throughout her house. Therefore, she did not see Constable Green leaving the building in triumph as he placed a carefully wrapped gun in his wagon. Franklin, on the other hand, could not help smirking as he opened the door for Green and the other detectives when they left the premises.

Believing the detectives had finished their job, Bevie slowly walked back toward the house where she unexpectedly met Constable Green coming toward her.

"We have concluded our search, Lady Beverley," he said stiffly. "The official inquest will be held at ten tomorrow morning at which time I expect to have a more complete summary of the cause of your father's death. Please be prompt. At the conclusion of the inquest, you will be free to go ahead with the arrangements for the funeral, but I must continue to insist that you remain at home. We will almost certainly have more questions for you."

Bevie offered him a regal nod after which he abruptly turned and left. She immediately informed Mrs. Metterson and the others that the funeral would be held in two days. "I shall be much relieved to have it over," she said with a dreary sigh. "It weighs heavily on my mind that Father has no permanent resting place."

Mr. Hydemark met with Bevie's solicitor that evening and proceeded to explain all of the latest clues he and Pick had uncovered. Mr. Styles listened intently as Hydemark told him of the bullet hole in the door, the footprints Mr. Pick had found under the library windows, and the notes from the strongbox. They discussed the upcoming inquest. The two men agreed to withhold the latest evidence to be used as ammunition in case Bevie should be tried for the crime.

"They have no other suspects," said Mr. Styles. "Scotland Yard is too busy to take serious interest in the case and the ineffective local chaps missed the most important clue as far as I can tell – that being the bullet hole in the door."

"Do you think the gambler, Colin Darley, plays into it?"

"I know him. He is rather a nice chap without any sense of when to leave the card tables. I doubt if he was involved, but we should not rule him out, certainly. Now, what about the small black book your friend found in the chair cushion?"

"Ah, yes, I nearly forgot. Mr. Pick is an astute fellow. He had the idea to call each of the household staff for an interview at which time he asked them to write down their name, position, and the amount they received each quarter. He told them that he wanted to be sure they were paid the correct amount. He already had that information, of course, but his aim was to secure a sample of their handwriting. Sadly, some of them were not able to write. However, Pick determined that the handwriting in the book belonged to Franklin, the butler.

"Very interesting. What is your understanding of the meaning of the entries in the book?"

"Mrs. Jackson, the housekeeper, revealed to me that she saw a box in the man's room where he hides his money. It seems odd that he should have so much more than his position would indicate and that he apparently feels compelled to take it out and count it frequently."

"Why not have a look in his room?"

"Do you think me a fool, Styles? He keeps it in a box with a false bottom. He has exactly the same amount of money in there as was written in the book, but no indication of where he got it."

"Perhaps he is a gambler."

"I think not. I believe he is carefully hiding it for a reason. Perhaps he is saving it up as bribe money, or it could be extortion money he has received."

"The latter sounds probable. What nasty gossip do you suppose he has encountered?"

"We shall sit near the front today, Lady Beverley. If they question you directly, you will defer to me for the answer. Keep your eyes looking straight ahead and do try to keep your head up regardless of any false accusations that come your way." These were a few of the instructions Mr. Styles imparted to Bevie.

A long table at the front of the room was occupied by one of the officers of The Queen's Household, an officer of H.M. Coroner for the district, Constable Green, two physicians who had attended the coroner, and the law writer.

The inquest was well underway and the findings were much the same as the preliminary inquest had been. That is, until Constable Green surprised the crowd with a statement about a gun that he had recovered from the bedroom of the accused. He pointed to Bevie.

The crowd gasped. Bevie was startled. She looked at Mr. Styles with an expression of terror. Mr. Styles was found wanting as far as any response was concerned.

Franklin stood up and shouted above the crowd. "I told ye she done it!"

Constable Green continued his diatribe. "As to whether or not one of the bullets can be matched to this weapon – it – I should say – well, the findings are inconclusive at this moment."

The audience shouted him down. "Off with you!" they screamed. "Let Scotland Yard find the answers! She done it. Hang her!"

Petra lurked in the doorway of the inquest, listening to the proceedings. She was dressed in an Italian peasant outfit with a scarf covering her head. When the people settled down, she made her grand entrance. Speaking in Italian with a few choice English words interspersed, she ran up the aisle shouting in a barely intelligible Italian accent, "Lady Beverley, Lady Beverley, where are you?"

The crowd silenced. The coroner was dumfounded. Constable Green stood up. "What is the meaning of this? Remove this peasant woman!"

Still no one stirred or moved toward Pet. "Oh my lady, you. . ." Here she began to rattle on in Italian as she fell on her knees in the aisle next to the row where Bevie sat.

Bevie stared at Pet with her mouth open while she struggled to prevent a giggle from escaping. After all, hadn't Mr. Styles instructed her to keep her head up and her eyes looking solemnly forward? The scene reminded her of the occasions when they had contrived a theater production in the dormitory at the finishing school in Switzerland.

Pet suddenly stood up and dramatically pointed at Franklin. She screamed hysterically, "Him was the one, him was the one what done it!"

The representative of Her Royal Majesty called for order and demanded that the girl be heard. Pet cowered in the front of the people and feigned ignorance of the English language as they asked her to explain her accusation. She rattled on in Italian, making no sense. Then she ran out of the building before anyone had gathered their wits enough to stop her.

It so disrupted the inquest that those in charge called for an end to the proceedings. Franklin was carted off to the constabulary for questioning. Mr. Styles took Bevie outside to the waiting carriage where Pet was hiding inside.

Mr. Hydemark joined them for the ride back to Burnside Court. He could not stop laughing. "Brava, brava," he kept repeating between howls.

"I would never have contrived such a distraction, but it seems to have had the intended effect," Mr. Styles said.

"You haven't changed a bit, Pet. I dare swear you should be an actress," Bevie added.

"I would dearly love to be on the stage, Bevie, but I cannot afford to ruin my sterling reputation. Why, no eligible bachelor would consider me."

"Hmmm, I thought you had sworn off men in general."

"Oh yes, darling, you are correct, but I nearly forgot my resolve when I caught a glimpse of that handsome young buck passing by the window of your sunroom."

Mr. Hydemark and Mr. Styles looked on with amusement.

"She means the accountant," Bevie whispered to Mr. Hydemark.

The day of the funeral dawned gray and dreary. Bevie sat in her room and refused to eat, drink, or see anyone but her abigail. She thought she would die of grief. When the time of the service drew near, Mr. Hydemark took it upon himself to burst into her room.

Bevie was shocked at his behavior. "It is highly improper for you to barge in here like this."

"Yes, I'm certain it is, but I felt it necessary to your well-being."

"How does your presence affect my well-being? I do appreciate your help, Mr. Hydemark, but this is preposterous."

"I believe it is time we spoke candidly about your spiritual condition. It seems to me that you are keeping God at bay and have done so for your entire life. Who, pray tell, do you believe He is?"

Bevie stared at the ceiling. "I suppose He is up there somewhere and that He did actually create the earth. It seems to me that He does whatever He chooses, including taking my father away from me."

"Everything you have said is true, however, you have done the very thing many people are inclined to do."

"Exactly what is that, Mr. Hydemark?"

"You have neglected to come to terms with your lost and sinful condition."

"What have I done that is so sinful? I did not kill my father if that is what you are implying."

"The Holy Scripture says that we have all sinned and, therefore, we fall short of the necessary requirements to enter heaven."

"Be that as it may, who am I to change what has been determined? It is our human condition."

"That is precisely where many people leave the subject. However, the good thing is that there is something to be done about it. The Scripture also says, 'For the wages of sin is death, but the gift of God is eternal life through Jesus Christ our Lord.'" Romans 6:23 (KJV)

"What exactly does that mean?"

"Simply that Christ died to pay the penalty for our sin and rose again so we might have eternal life. On that awful day, he took our sin upon Himself that we might have the hope of spending eternity with Him."

". . . and what must we do to obtain such a gift, Mr. Hydemark?"

"I can only say what the Scriptures tell us in the Book of Romans, '…if thou shalt confess with thy mouth the Lord Jesus, and shalt believe in thine heart that God hath raised him from the dead, thou shalt be saved. For with the heart man believeth unto righteousness; and with the mouth confession is made unto salvation. For the scripture saith, whosoever believeth on him shall not be ashamed.'" Romans 10:9-11 (KJV)

"I will consider what you have said, Mr. Hydemark, but just now I must dress for my father's burial."

Mr. Hydemark bowed and left the room, gently closing the door.

Petra's brother, Nicolo, accompanied Pet to the funeral. Bevie hung between Nicolo and Pet, leaning on Pet's arm the entire time. She was distraught and barely attended to the service or to those who were present. Pet guided her throughout the ordeal, telling her when to speak to someone and leading her away whenever possible.

When at last they returned to the house for refreshments, Petra took Bevie to her room and insisted that she compose herself long enough to greet some of the guests.

"It is highly irregular of you to ignore those who have come to pay their respects," Pet admonished her. "Wash your face and change into another gown. It is important that you take your place in this house. I do not want that silly man and his mother thinking they are going to take over here and stay well beyond what is considered polite and normative."

"Yes, I had forgotten about them. I suppose my father's man of law, Mr. Desford, is on the scene, is he not?"

"I have never met the gentleman, but I will inquire if you wish."

"Yes do, Pet, thank you."

"I expect you to be ready to greet the guests when I return."

"I promise. Will you kindly ask Susie to attend me?"

It was a monumental mountain for Bevie to scale. She somehow had to pull herself together. She did not want to disgrace her father's name in any way. She splashed water on her face several times and tried to apply some creams in order to make herself presentable. Suzie helped her with a fresh gown. It seemed only a few minutes until Pet returned. She was not alone.

"Mr. Desford has not arrived. Mr. Pick said he is expected tomorrow or the next day. I have brought Nicolo up here to escort you to the dining area. It always looks well if you have a strong and handsome man at your side when things are difficult."

Nicolo bowed and said, "I understand that this day is very difficult and I will be honored to help in any way. May I escort you and stay by your side? I promise to remain in the background, but handy if you should need a shoulder to lean on."

Bevie hardly noticed the tall, dark-haired man standing beside her. His dark eyes had a flicker of gold in them and his kind expression was the only thing Bevie registered in her grief-stricken state. "It is very kind of you, Mr. Gabrieli. I am most grateful since I find it difficult to negotiate the crowd on my own."

"Please call me Nicky."

"Yes, and I give you leave to call me Bevie if you wish."

Bevie took his arm and the three of them went into the ballroom where the guests were beginning to gather. The tables were spread with abundant food of all kinds. Vases of white flowers were placed discreetly and artfully on the tables. Bevie was unaware of the increased burden that had been placed on Mrs. Metterson and the staff to have arranged and prepared the lavish spread suitable for an earl's funeral, but Pet noticed and made a mental note to tell Bevie that she should especially thank all of them.

When at last it was over and only the houseguests remained, Mr. Hydemark suggested that Pet, Nicky, Mr. Pick, and Mrs. Metterson meet him in the drawing room for tea or coffee. Bevie hesitated, but he explained that he had something important to say. They all headed toward the drawing room and found Cecil and Araminta there as usual.

"Thank you for coming," Mrs. Metterson said to them. "Will you need any help packing your things? I suppose you will be leaving on the morrow."

Cecil immediately got his hackles up. "I will have you know that I am now the sixth Earl of Burnside. It is my duty to remain until the reading of the will and beyond, if necessary. I will be making some long-overdue changes in this household, I assure you, madam," he announced with his familiar sneer.

Mr. Hydemark stepped into the scuffle. "My good man, how generous it is of you to remain here for such a *very long* time. I am certain it has become quite tedious for both you and Mrs. Busslingthorpe. However, since the title has not yet been legally passed down and, indeed, the distribution of assets not yet made, please excuse us while we confer on some personal matters."

Cecil was fuming, but managed to bite his tongue as he entertained ideas of what he would do to each one of them when he reigned as the sixth Earl of Burnside. He stiffly bowed and took his mother out of the room.

"Stuffy old bag of wind," Pet commented.

"Shhhh," Mrs. Metterson put her finger to her lips. She quietly moved to the door, flung it open, and came face to face with Cecil. "Is there something else, Mr. Busslingthorpe?" she asked the chagrinned eavesdropper.

"I was just – I wanted – never mind," he said, turning away.

She closed the door amidst snickering from the others.

"You certainly must have the keenest hearing of anyone I've ever met. It is the second time I've seen you do that," Bevie noted.

"It isn't my hearing at all, my dear girl. It is only that I have spent some time observing human behavior – sinners that we all are."

Sinners – we are all sinners – the words struck Bevie and resonated in her head.

"Now then, let us call for tea and then I shall disclose our latest information," said Mr. Hydemark.

They discussed the day's events until the maid delivered a tray with tea, coffee, cheese, and some confections. She quickly left the room.

"Here is the latest development," Mr. Hydemark began. "Henry Pick has conferred with Lord Burnside's bank and carefully compared the account books with the bank accounts. I am very disturbed to have to relate to you that there is a wide discrepancy in the figures. It seems that someone has gone off with a considerable amount of the earl's money."

A unified gasp filled the room.

"Who?" They asked in unison.

"It can only be surmised that Mr. Edwin Hughes, Burnside's man of business, was the guilty party. Unfortunately, as most of you know, he appears to have vanished into thin air after declaring his intention to attend the bedside of a dying relative in Spain. However, I can safely say through reliable sources, that he has been observed on two occasions enjoying the sun and sand in the South of France. I have taken the liberty of informing Constable Green of this finding."

Another gasp ensued.

"That is most appalling," shot out Mrs. Metterson. "I took it that he was a loyal employee of the late Lord Burnside."

"He had only been with us for a few months," Bevie added. "Still, I have never known any of our staff to be so dishonest."

"Yes, I am afraid it is in our base nature to be such," added Henry.

It is our nature to be dishonest – all sinners. The words accosted Bevie's conscience again.

"What is to be done?" asked Pet.

Henry Pick smiled broadly at her. He had heard that the dark-haired beauty thought he was handsome. "Now we have only to await the arrival of the solicitor. Our next action will, of course, depend upon the distribution of the estate and the new earl."

Mr. Hydemark stood up and walked toward the door. "I believe that is all I have to say at this time. Thank you all for joining me here."

Bevie was confused, weary and disturbed, but could not imagine resting under such trying circumstances. A loud sigh escaped.

"I suggest we all stroll around the gardens. Perhaps it will be relaxing after a difficult day," Pet offered.

"Thank you, but I must tend to some work," said Mrs. Metterson.

"I must ask to be excused as well," added Mr. Hydemark.

That left the two couples who naturally fell in step with one another.

"Where will you go if that abrasive chap inherits everything?" Nicky asked Bevie.

"I have not been able to think that far ahead. My mind seems to be determined to stay in a muddle."

"She will come and stay with us at your townhouse, Nicky," suggested Pet.

"I could never impose on you in such a way, even if there were a suitable chaperone in the house. I suppose I shall try to find a position – governess or some such thing."

The four stopped by the garden fountain. "I feel certain your father will have provided for you, Lady Beverley. According to his books, he maintains several properties," Henry offered.

"Yes, there is the one in Scotland and one down by the sea somewhere."

"I understand he also has a hunting box. Was he a hunter, Lady Beverley?"

"No, Mr. Pick, he did not hunt, but he kept it for his friends who enjoy the sport. I went with him to visit the place a few years ago and found it to be cold, isolated, and very sparse. I sincerely hope his will does not indicate that I am to live there. I should freeze to death."

"It would be an unusual thing for a father to leave his daughter a hunting lodge as her primary residence."

Franklin angrily snuffed out his cigar, mindless of the fact that he had now stolen two boxes of them from the library at Burnside Court. "How long 'er ye keepin' me here?" he inquired of the clerk at the constabulary.

"I think 'till you tell 'em what they already know – that you're a rotter."

"Shut yer trap. Yer nothing but a blimy, rag-tag nobody."

The clerk walked away, but not before he said, "You'll sing – see if you don't."

He did sing – and quite soon after the clerk left and not more than five minutes after Constable Green told him that Hughes had confessed to the "whole match" which, of course, Hughes had not and, in fact, was still at large.

"I ain't done nuthin', constable. He paid me to keep my mouth shut about him and his friend fixin' the books and I did. What's the crime in that?"

"Let us imagine that taking a bribe is no crime, but that Hughes wanted Burnside dead so he wouldn't find out about the stolen money. Let us say that he agreed to pay you a handsome sum to do the chap in, see? Now that would be a crime, wouldn't it? How did you do it, Franklin? Did you shoot him, poison him, or both?"

Beads of sweat rolled down Franklin's face. "I swear to ye, Constable, I didn't do him in."

"If you did not, who did? Did you hire an assassin? Come now, Franklin, we've got you pegged. It could go easier for you if you would only confess."

Franklin saw his holiday in France disappearing before his eyes. He tried to think of some way to implicate another person who could have done it. Hughes was out of sight when Burnside was murdered, so it could not have been him. "I – I saw that viscount's nephew hide the gun in the girl's room. It's what happened, but I was afraid to say. Them peers have a way of pushin' the blame on us lowers, you know, gov."

"Do you speak of William Henderson, then?"

"That's him – the neighbor."

"That is very interesting, Franklin, but it does not absolve you in the least. I am compelled to keep you here until the mystery of this crime is solved."

Constable Green summoned an officer to escort Franklin to his cell.

CHAPTER SIX

Nicky tucked Bevie's hand into the crook of his arm as they walked toward the house. He thought she was lovely, but he had never entertained the idea of spending time with one woman, let alone one of her class. His previous romantic interests had been deliberately limited to women who were not interested in that awful state of marriage. He had promised his sister that he would attempt to help Bevie get her feet on the ground during this chaotic time. After that, he would make some excuse to disappear into his chosen society.

Romance was the furthest thing from Bevie's mind. In fact, it had always been a distant consideration in that she had too many interesting things she wished to accomplish before she thought of settling into what she deemed to be the boring lifestyle of the married.

Cecil Busslingthorpe assumed that every woman of Bevie's age was frantically trying to make a good match. He and his mother sat in her room discussing the situation.

"If it should happen that old Burnside fixed it so that the estate is free and not entailed, you could very well find yourself with a title and no money, dear boy," Araminta said thoughtfully. "I do not wish that for you."

"Nor do I, Mother. What shall I do? I could marry the girl now as a precaution in the event that I do not inherit the lands, but what of Lady Mary? We are pledged."

"You cannot chance waiting, my love. You must understand that if Lady Beverley does inherit all the money and lands, it will be too late for you to engage her affection. She would suspect you of being a fortune hunter. On the other hand, if you were to marry her now with the heartfelt excuse that you wish to protect her from all of these accusations, the money would be yours either way."

"I cannot do that to Lady Mary. We have plans to marry."

"You will just have to find a way to get rid of your first wife as soon as it is expedient. Many have done it before you. Goodness knows your father tried, but failed to detach himself from me."

"You never told me exactly how he fell into the ravine, Mother."

"It was a terrible accident. I cannot bear to speak of it."

Cecil did not press her to explain. "I had hoped things would go smoothly when we came to Burnside Court. When will that idiot solicitor arrive?"

"The latest news is that he will be here next week. You have one week to make this right, Cecil. I am counting on you."

When no one came to greet him, Constable Green pounded harder on the front door of Glenarm Place. Carter pulled on his jacket as he hurried down the front hallway.

"Hold on. Who's calling at this ungodly hour?" he mumbled as he reluctantly opened the door.

"I am here to speak with Lord Sedley and his nephew," growled Constable Green.

"As you can imagine, constable, the household is not yet stirring. Could you not wait until a decent hour?"

"Get them down here now or I'll find them myself."

Carter led Constable Green to the drawing room and went to make an attempt at rousting William out of his bed. Lord Sedley was already up and heard the commotion.

When William learned that Constable Green had made a special trip to see them at the awful hour of nine on the clock, he jumped out of bed and began rehearsing the story he had prepared. His hand shook as he dressed. He took in deep breaths in an attempt to calm his pounding heart. He stumbled and barely caught himself before he fell headlong down the steps.

Lord Sedley was first to greet the constable. "Your early visit is quite unusual, Green. I hope nothing else untoward has happened in the neighborhood."

"Not that I can say, Lord Sedley. Please sit down. We have some things to discuss as soon as your nephew makes an appearance."

"I see. Would you mind terribly if we went to the breakfast room and spoke over coffee?"

"If you feel that we must, but I don't have time to dilly-dally over crumpets."

Once they were seated and the coffee poured, Constable Green plunged into the subject. "We have reason to believe that the gun found inside Burnside Court belonged to you or your nephew."

Sedley was at a loss to understand. "I was not aware that one of our guns was missing, Constable. May I inquire as to which gun you found?"

William entered the room at that moment, poured himself a cup of coffee, and sat down next to his uncle. He tried to look puzzled.

"Are you aware that one of our guns is missing, William?"

"No, why? Has there been a thief afoot?"

Constable Green leaned toward William. "Someone fitting your description was observed hiding the gun in Lady Beverley's room."

William stood up. "See here now, Constable. I have never set foot in the lady's boudoir."

"We have a witness, sir."

"A false one, I assure you."

"Let us stop all this nonsense and go down to the gun room and prove once and for all that none of our guns are missing," said Lord Sedley.

William dragged behind as the two others walked briskly over the frayed carpet to the east wing. He tried to imagine who had found the gun, removed it to Bevie's room, and then proceeded to implicate him in the murder. He had only planned to make it look as though someone from Burnside Court had stolen the gun, used it on Burnside, and then hid it in the garden shed.

Lord Sedley was stunned. "I am at a loss to know what to say, Constable. One of our hunting guns seems to be missing. It, in fact, is one of my prized hunting guns."

"One and the same, Lord Sedley."

"What are the circumstances under which you learned of the presence of the gun?"

"I choose not to disclose the particulars of the on-going investigation, Lord Sedley, but I will have to take William down to headquarters for questioning."

William's eyes appealed to his uncle for help.

"Now just a minute, Constable," Sedley said heatedly. "We have a right to know who has accused William of such a monstrous crime."

"Very well, sir, I suppose you do have the right. It was Burnside's butler, Franklin."

"That liar!" interjected William. "He no doubt stole the gun and murdered the dear man himself."

"That could be the case, Mr. Henderson, but we need all the facts. Now gather your things and come along with me."

"Uncle. . ."

"If he is being dragged into your den, Constable, then I shall be there as well," Sedley said sternly.

"If you insist, sir."

Bevie sat at her escritoire writing notes of thanks when Suzie came to announce that Mr. Busslingthorpe wished to see her.

"Hasn't that creature left the house, yet? Tell him I shall meet him in the sunroom at quarter past the hour."

When she finally dragged herself into the sunroom, Cecil jumped up and hurried toward her with outstretched hands. "My dear girl, you must be utterly exhausted."

"As a matter of fact, I am. What is it you wished to see me about, Mr. Busslingthorpe?"

"As you might imagine, I have had hours and hours to think about the terrible things that are happening to you. I only wish to make your life more comfortable. It has occurred to me that there might be something I can do or say to convince the authorities of your innocence. It is my greatest wish that you should have no worries at this juncture in your life."

"I do not believe there is a thing anyone can do unless you care to admit guilt yourself."

"Now that is certainly outrageous. How would anyone believe such a thing when I was not within miles of this place when the tragedy occurred?"

"It might interest you to learn that someone espied you not three miles from here on that very day."

Cecil was speechless for longer than he should have been. "People are easily mistaken for others, are they not?"

It was the first time Bevie had even suspected that Cecil might actually have had something to do with her father's murder. She had only told the lie to throw him off.

Even as she lied, her conscience accused her. *We are all sinners – it is in our very nature.* "Exactly where were you on that day, Mr. Busslingthorpe?"

"Now, now, my dear, you are no doubt overwrought. Please allow me to take you into the gardens. A leisurely stroll will serve to calm your nerves." He slipped her hand into the crook of his arm and nearly dragged her through the outside door of the sunroom. She decided to go along without objection. She had the most unusual feeling that he might have done the terrible deed.

When Cecil returned to the drawing room where his mother waited for word of his success, he told her of Bevie's accusation.

"Dear me, that is something I never expected," she said.

"Why would anyone expect it, Mother?"

"I only meant that I believed her to be a . . . mouse of sorts."

"What shall I do now?"

"Move quickly with your courtship, son. If she does not respond within two days, you must outright plead with her to marry you and save her own skin. Tell her that as sixth Earl of Burnside, you will have the power to fend off the law. Say anything – only make her see that she must marry you."

Mr. Hydemark met Bevie as she turned the corner to ascend the stairs. "How are you, dear girl?"

"I am still numb. I suppose it is better to be numb than in great pain."

"God will comfort you if you will only let Him."

"I would welcome some real comfort, Mr. Hydemark. That snake, Busslingthorpe, pretends to comfort me when I know he wants something else – perhaps any money I might inherit. Do you know, I think he may have killed my father?"

"What could make you accuse him of murder?"

"In jest I mentioned – well, actually I told a lie. I believe you may be right about my being a sinner. At any rate, when Cecil said he wanted to make my life comfortable, I suggested that he could if he were to confess to committing the crime. Then I told him someone had seen him not three miles from here on the day of the murder. He stumbled for words, but never denied it."

"That is certainly a new twist on things."

Araminta searched long and hard for a solution to her son's problem. She paced the floor in front of the chair where he sat dozing.

Finally she said, "Wake up, son. I have just recalled an appointment with my surgeon. You know how I suffer from the headaches. In fact, I have a dreadful one just now. However, I do not wish for these people to think I am out of sorts. I must return home for a day or so. In the meantime, you must make excuses as though I were indisposed and keeping to my room. Do not allow anyone to go inside or discover that I am elsewhere. You must act as though you occasionally attend me. Do you understand?"

"Yes, Mother, but why can't I come with you? I would dearly love to see Lady Mary before I take the next step with Beverley. I want to explain to her why it is necessary for me to do so."

"Try to think clearly! You cannot afford to waste a minute in your courtship of Lady Beverley. You must stay here and guard your rightful place."

"Alright, Mother, but only if you will allow me to send a missive to Lady Mary."

"Make haste, then, and when you finish writing, ask someone if you might drive Burnside's enclosed conveyance to fetch my medicine from the apothecary since it is raining. You will take me to the place where I can board the omnibus that will take me to our home."

Lord Sedley, being an important Member of Parliament, was able to convince Constable Green that he would take responsibility to see that William stayed close to home. Thus, William was free. The first thing he did upon arriving at Glenarm Place was to put on his riding clothes and make way for Burnside Court where he intended to convince Bevie to marry him.

If they were married when it was discovered that the bullet from his gun killed her father, she would be his wife and the courts would likely believe it was an accident and acquit him, he reasoned.

When he arrived, it was to find Bevie in the drawing room arguing with Cecil Busslingthorpe about borrowing her father's carriage – which she finally allowed.

"Pardon the intrusion, Bevie, but it was my understanding that we were to go riding this afternoon," he lied.

Bevie was not in the mood to ride with William, but she felt it would be far better than having to spend time with the arrogant Busslingthorpe.

"Of course, William, I have only been delayed," she said, glaring at Cecil. "I shall be ready in a few moments. I must change into my riding habit." *There is another lie – one from William and another from me- sinners that we all are!*

As Bevie and William rode toward the meadow adjacent to Sedley's property, William slowed his pace and reined his horse in next to Bevie.

"Let's walk over toward the stream. It is the first clear day we have enjoyed in a long time and I need to stretch my legs," William said as he dismounted and then helped Bevie to do the same.

"It is much too cold for my liking. I am impatient for spring and blooms and warm breezes."

"Has it not been the most trying winter of all? I am so very sorry about Lord Burnside. How are you able to bear it, Bevie?"

She felt relaxed for the first time since the murder. Riding along with William took her back to her childhood days when they had run across the very meadow where they were now walking together. She had to admit those were good times and she could almost forgive William for becoming such a goose.

They walked until they came to an ancient stone wall that was tumbling down. There they sat on a pile of rocks that had worn smooth from years of pelting rain. William sat close to Bevie and moved in for the attack.

"I've been doing a great deal of thinking since that terrible day, Bev. It has been too unbelievably awful for such a beautiful creature as you to have to endure all that has happened. Certainly you understand how fond I am of you – and have been since we raced across these fields as children. Please come away with me, Bev, and I will make your troubles disappear. By the time we return, things will not seem so grim. I shall take you to Spain, Switzerland, or even America if you wish. Say you will marry me."

Bevie jerked her head around to look squarely at him. "What are you saying, William?"

"I am asking you to be my wife."

Bevie was so taken by surprise that she could not think of a response. Fortunately, it was not necessary for her to do so. A rider came charging toward them at break-neck speed and stopped just in front of where they sat. It was one of the stable boys from Burnside Court.

The boy slid off the horse and bowed before Bevie. "Yer pardon, Lady Beverley. Constable Green is at the 'ouse and wants you 'mediatly. He came to the stables, shoutin' for me to get you."

"I'll be right there, Kit. Tell Franklin to appease him with a drink."

"Yes, miss," he said as he flew up on the horse and rode away.

All thoughts of answering William without hurting his feelings were forgotten as Bevie hurried back to her horse and returned to the house.

Hydemark walked into the library where Henry Pick leaned back in the chair behind the desk. "He's here again – Constable Green, I mean. What do you suppose he wants this time?"

"Well, from what I can gather, he doesn't know what he wants. He's got – let me see – five or six suspects and nothing certain. No doubt they haven't proven that Sedley's gun did it or they would have carted him off to gaol. Then there is Hughes, Franklin, poor Lady Beverley, and now the possibility of Busslingthorpe."

"Green hasn't yet thought of the last possibility and don't forget the fact that they questioned his mother."

"That, of course, seems odd. What do you think about her?"

"She seems desperate to make her home here, does she not?"

"I would have to agree. My concern just now is that Green is disposed to blame Lady Beverley no matter the facts."

"Rest easy, my friend. Do not forget that we have some interesting clues that Green has not discovered in case she should be brought to trial," Pick assured Hydemark.

"What about the poison? What was the purpose of poisoning and shooting the poor soul twice?"

Pick rubbed his forehead. "A very good question, Hydemark. Shall we put our minds to the task of discovering a reason?"

"We must first assume the poison came through food or drink and may have been administered by one of the servants."

"Who better than Franklin?"

"Perhaps."

"I am sorry to interrupt you, gentlemen, but I have been summoned from my ride and am forced to endure the company of Constable Green as though it were an emergency," Bevie said between gasps for breath. "Would the two of you mind coming to my rescue once more? I fear he is up to no good and I am so confused that I hardly know how to regard him."

Hydemark spoke up. "We shall come immediately and I would advise you to say as little as possible. I believe the man is grasping for some way to solve the crime. He now has some powerful men putting pressure on him to do so."

"Knowing that fact does not comfort me at all, Mr. Hydemark."

"Nevertheless, my dear girl, he is bound to try to accuse someone whether he has any kind of proof or not. Keep that in mind and be very evasive with your answers."

The three entered the drawing room expecting to encounter Cecil and his mother as well as Constable Green. The former two were conspicuously absent. Constable Green stood up.

Bevie nodded and Constable Green made no attempt to return the courtesy. Bevie kept standing, thereby indicating that she had no time for the constable.

"I fear I have some bad news for you, Lady Beverley," he said.

"Please do not keep us waiting with your news, Constable," Bevie clipped.

"We have concluded that you are the most likely suspect to have killed your father."

"What basis do you have for this absurd conclusion?"

"I am not at liberty to say at the moment."

Mr. Hydemark stepped forward. "On the contrary, Green, I am well aware of the law. If you have a particular accusation to make against this lady, then tell us by what means you have come to this conclusion. Otherwise, I must ask that you stop this eternal nuisance you seem to have created simply because you do not have a viable suspect."

Constable Green's eyes narrowed with hate. "You are not above the law, Hydemark, and I advise you to watch your words." He turned to Bevie and said, "Tell me again why you were in the library at the time of your father's murder."

"I was not."

Hydemark smiled.

Henry Pick said, "Hmmm, I recall that we've been over this a thousand times, Green. Perhaps you would be so kind as to tell Lady Beverley just exactly what new evidence you have uncovered."

"Who are you?"

"Henry Pick, Lady Beverley's accountant. It seems to me you have overlooked the fact that the butler has taken a bribe to keep silent concerning some underhanded theft of considerable importance here at Burnside Court. Perhaps you should be seeking the whereabouts of the thief. That would appear to be a likely direction for your investigation, would it not?"

"What do bean counters know of the law? Keep to your profession, Pick."

"Oh, I shall, I shall. Perhaps you could – um – brush up on yours a bit, Constable."

Constable Green moved toward the doorway. "I am not finished here, Lady Beverley – not by a long shot. I'll see you at the constabulary again before this investigation has finished." He stomped out the door.

Bevie was dumfounded. "You were positively splendid. Thank you so much – both of you."

Hydemark laughed. "Good work, Henry."

Pet crashed through the front door with her usual aplomb. The under butler came running to the entrance when he heard the intruder. "Please wait, miss," he cried as Pet merely smiled, waved him away, and continued on her way toward the drawing room.

"I heard all of you laughing in here. I just passed that tweedy detective fellow hurrying away from the house. I hope you are in a state of mirth because of some happy news at last."

"Hello, my dear friend," Bevie exclaimed. "It is only that Mr. Hydemark and Mr. Pick have given him a set down that would make anyone smile."

"I can well believe it. Both of you are absolutely to be admired for your quick wit and humor."

Henry's chest rose and inflated involuntarily. He nearly always found himself speechless in the presence of the dark-haired beauty. He felt like a simpleton when his most elegant smile would not recede simply due to her speaking to him.

Pet returned the smile. "Why Mr. Pick, I was wondering if you would ever find time to leave this dreary house. Nearly a week has gone by now and I do believe you are in need of some air. Come, all of you. We must take advantage of the blue skies since we all know that England cannot bear to allow us to enjoy many of them."

"Do I gather that your home is in Italy where the sun shines most readily, Miss Gabrieli?" Mr. Hydemark inquired.

"More or less. I was born in Milan, but my parents are musicians and travel the world, you see. Because of that, I have never lived in one place for more than a year. I suppose you may think me a gypsy."

Henry wanted to say that he thought her beautiful, but his tongue was fastened to the roof of his mouth.

"I suppose William is waiting for me since I left him in a hurry when that dreadful constable summoned me. I'll see if he is in the sun room. If you walk slowly, we shall soon meet you on the path leading to the folly," Bevie suggested.

"Forgive my old legs for crying off," said Mr. Hydemark. I believe I'll take advantage of the quiet and sit in the conservatory – or perhaps lie down on that soft couch by the orange trees."

Henry could not believe it when he found himself alone with Pet. She took his arm and they sauntered along the path amidst the spring flowers that were just beginning to break through the ground.

"I wondered if you would agree to dine at my brother's home this evening, Mr. Pick. He is thinking of having a few friends in for dinner and a rubber of whist. Mr. Hydemark is invited as well, of course," she quickly added.

"I – I – w – w – would be de – delighted."

"I wonder if it would be wrong of me to ask Bevie to come. I know that odious constable has ordered her to stay at home, but I cannot see that it would matter if she were to come for an evening. Would he even know?"

"I – that is – umm. . ."

"Oh thank you, Mr. Pick. I knew you could arrange it. Come in the barouche and no one will suspect she has left the house. Of course, you will have to make excuses to that awful Mr. Busslingthorpe and his mother."

Suddenly, Mr. Pick forgot his shyness. "Good heavens, I haven't seen Busslingthorpe or his mother for quite some time. I can only hope they have at last gone away."

"Here are Bevie and William. Please do not mention my brother's little entertainment in front of that young man," begged Pet.

"I would not think of it."

At eight o'clock that evening, Nicky welcomed Bevie, Henry Pick, Mr. Hydemark, and Mrs. Metterson to his home. Pet stood regally by, making the perfect hostess. Mr. Hydemark would have begged off in order to keep a close watch on things at Burnside Court, but he was anxious to observe Nicolo Gabrieli and his sister, Petra. During the evening, he relaxed his watch, being convinced that they did not suddenly appear on the scene to make trouble for Bevie.

Bevie had given her maid, Suzie, particular instructions concerning her whereabouts that evening in the event that any of the nosey houseguests or one of the staff should inquire. Suzie was to let it be known that Bevie had decided to retire early and did not wish to be disturbed. Suzie was quite happy with the arrangement and quickly made plans for a secret assignation during Bevie's absence.

Bevie was looking especially beautiful in a gown of azure blue with a narrow band of white lace at the neckline. Nicky was mesmerized by her. It was nothing especially new for him since he had forever admired beautiful women of all ages.

During the course of the evening, Nicky guided Bevie into a corner where he quietly reiterated his willingness to secretly scuttle her off to the Continent should a trial be on the horizon. "I have many friends who would help us and several little villas that would make perfect hiding places," he assured her.

"And what of the future when I wish to return to my homeland?" she asked.

"We must assume the authorities will have captured the real villain by that time."

"I suppose that must be true, but I have a particular aversion to running away from life's problems."

"You have much courage, but when a brick wall is up against you and you have nowhere to go, you must reach for a helping hand, no?"

He always made her laugh with his slightly garbled and unique way of speaking English. "I will keep the offer at the forefront of my thinking and I thank you for your trust."

They quit the secluded corner of the room and joined the others just as the tea tray was brought in at ten o'clock. Pet poured coffee and tea as each one wished. Later they engaged in a lively game of whist. The group from Burnside Court did not return home until just after one in the morning.

Bevie was exasperated when she rang for Suzie and she did not appear. She assumed she had fallen asleep. After twisting and turning, she managed to unbutton the many buttons on the back of her dress and slip out of her stays.

CHAPTER SEVEN

Mrs. Araminta Busslingthorpe dispatched a note to her son informing him of the approximate time of her return to Burnside Court. This was done at considerable risk to her credibility in that someone might chance to intercept the missive and discover her to be out rather than confined to her room.

Cecil, in receipt of the missive, did not ask to borrow the carriage for the second time when it became necessary to meet his mother, since he failed to think of a viable excuse to present to the lady of the house. Instead, he walked one mile down the road where he was fortunate to be able to hail the driver of a hack who agreed to take him to the place where the omnibus would deposit Araminta. He retained the hired hack which eventually carried mother and son back to the place where Cecil had first secured the driver.

"I do not wish to walk a mile in the dark, Cecil. Why must we alight so soon?"

"That should not be so difficult to understand, Mother. You asked me to spread the word that you were sadly indisposed and refused to leave your room. How then would we explain it when you arrived at the front entrance in a hack?"

"Yes, of course, but I hate for you to have to carry my heavy bag such a great distance."

"I shall manage. Did you see your physician?"

"What? Oh yes, of course I did."

"And are you feeling well?"

"Quite well, thank you, son."

"I have done some thinking while you were away, Mother. I have decided that the uppity Lady Beverley will not accept my suit. She has been vehemently opposed to any advances I have made in that direction. So, it seems that I shall be required to find another means of assuring that I am the recipient of the vast portion of the estate in the event that it is not entailed."

"What do you propose, dear boy?"

"Simply get rid of her."

"An excellent idea, but we cannot murder her in cold blood without drawing suspicion our way."

"Perhaps we could send her off somewhere and spread the rumor that she took flight due to her guilt."

"Let me think about what you suggest, Cecil. Perhaps things will work for our good in the near future – and do not forget that you may well inherit it all."

The two need not have hidden in the garden until after midnight since no one of import would have seen them entering the house. However, just as they were going along the north wall beside the servant's entrance, they heard the approach of a carriage. They quickly moved out of sight and watched as Bevie and her entourage stepped out of the barouche and quickly disappeared in the direction of the kitchen entrance.

"Well now," said Cecil, "I wonder what Constable Green will say when he learns that little miss uppity has left the house in direct defiance of his orders."

"Let us tuck that bit of information away until exactly the right moment, Cecil."

"Just as you say, Mother."

Bevie had barely dropped off into a sound sleep when she was awakened suddenly. She sat up in bed pondering what might have startled her. As she listened, she realized the wind had begun to blow. She heard the banging of the shutters and she momentarily relaxed. A moment later, she heard angry voices coming from somewhere below her window. It brought her to her feet. The sounds were somewhat muffled by the noise of the wind.

Curious to discover the identity of the people, she drew the curtains aside and opened her window. In the darkness, she could make out two figures – a man and a woman – who were flailing arms and fists at each other in a fit of rage. Believing it to be two of the servants, she called down for them to cease their arguing and go to their beds at once. The man fled and the woman disappeared under the overhang of the roof where Bevie could not view her direction.

Sleep was gone and Bevie lay staring into the darkness, thinking about the ways in which her life had changed dramatically since her father's death. Until recently, she had seemingly floated along with whatever came her way and never bothered to be concerned about anything other than new gowns, hats, and her horses.

Now, she realized, she must begin to take some sort of charge of herself and point her life in a meaningful direction. That was the simple truth, but the means of doing it eluded her. She wondered if Mr. Hydemark was correct in his assessment of humankind and that she was, after all, a miserable sinner with no hope. She decided that she must talk to the vicar and ask his advice. Then she remembered what a hopeless bore his sermons were and decided against it.

As rays of light began to shine through the curtains, she slid out of bed and donned her riding habit. She had just left her room when her quiet steps were arrested by sounds coming from Suzie's room. She knocked lightly and then entered without an invitation. She found her maid sobbing in her bed.

"Is something amiss, Suzie? What is it?"

"It is nothing, miss."

"Please allow me to help if I may."

"Oh miss, I have to confess that I was out seeing someone in the town last night. We had a right awful disagreement. That is what it was."

"I see. Was it you I heard arguing beneath my window, then?"

"Yes, miss."

"Who is the gentleman, Suzie – or should I say, who is the reckless toad that dares to treat you thus?"

"You don't know him. I will be alright, miss. Do you need me to help you this morning?"

"I suggest that you keep to your bed until I return from a short ride. I also think you should end your dangerous assignations with that man."

Bevie turned and left the room. She was quite angry with Suzie. She had believed her to be above such clandestine meetings. A thought came to her unbidden. *We are all sinners – it is our nature.*

Kit, the stable boy, heard Bevie's approach and climbed down from his bunk, pulling on his breeches and coat as he hurried to saddle Serenity for her ride.

"You needn't have come, Kit. I could have done for myself. Serenity is such a docile creature."

"Never, my lady. It is my pleasure to serve you."

"Thank you, Kit. You are a fine boy and I hope you will come with me if I am ousted from this house."

"Why would that happen, miss?"

"Well, if Mr. Busslingthorpe takes ownership of the estate, he will no doubt toss me out. I trust that I will not lose my horses and that you will be the one to help me take care of them."

"I do want to, miss, and I hope that cove gets nothin'."

"I'm ashamed to say that I hope so, too."

Once she was away from the house, she began to relax and enjoy the early morning mist. When she came to the meadow where she and William had stopped, she dismounted and walked to the wall where they sat when he proposed marriage. She began to wonder if she would be better off accepting his suit since she felt at loose ends and quite hopeless.

She thought of praying, but in the next moment thought better of it since she was beginning to believe that she was a flagrant sinner and that God must be angry with her. In fact, she decided her failures were the reason God had taken her father away.

Not quite having reached the point of doing something about her sinful state, her thoughts were suddenly interrupted and her attention drawn to a rustling in the wooded area beyond where she sat. She stood quickly as her eyes roamed over the area seeking the cause of the noise and, at the same time, she hurried toward her horse in case it should be a wild animal ready to do harm to Serenity.

Not a minute had passed when she observed a man running in the opposite direction from where she stood. "Hail there! Who are you?" she called.

He kept running and she realized she had been wrong to go riding without the presence of a groom or, at the very least, another person. When she returned to the house, she found everything in an uproar.

Mrs. Metterson came running to meet her. "Where have you been, Bevie? I have been beside myself thinking something untoward had happened to you."

"I am so sorry, Mrs. Metterson. I did not wish to disturb the household at such an early hour."

"Nevertheless, you must hurry and prepare for a visit from Lord Burnside's solicitor, Mr. Desford. He has sent word that he is to arrive this morning!"

"Oh dear, I fear I am not ready to receive anyone, much less hear what dreadful circumstances await my future. Where is Mr. Hydemark?"

"Here I am," he said as he came to meet her. "You have nothing to fear as far as living arrangements are concerned, my dear girl. Mrs. Metterson and I will make certain you are well settled in some worthy home."

"That is very kind of you, but I must find my own way in the world now that my father has left me. What time do we expect Mr. Desford?"

The question was left hanging as Cecil appeared on the scene. "What? Desford is here? Why have I not been notified?"

"Calm down, Bustlethorn," Henry Pick scolded, deliberately mispronouncing his name. "We have just now received word of his visit."

"I say, what have you to do with anything? You don't belong here and have no business barging into the family affairs."

"Perhaps not, but at the very least I came by invitation."

"Must we quarrel in front of the servants?" Mrs. Metterson interrupted. "It is in very poor taste as you all know very well."

Bevie had barely finished changing into her morning gown when she heard the under-butler announce the arrival of Mr. Desford. She hurried down the stairs, not bothering to allow Suzie to arrange her hair which was bouncing on her shoulders as she descended the steps. Mr. Hydemark met her and whispered that the solicitor was in the library waiting for her.

Her lip quivered. "I am very nervous."

"No need, dear girl," he said as he tucked her hand under his arm and escorted her into the library.

Mr. Desford stood and greeted Bevie with a bow. "I am truly devastated to learn of the unhappy events of the past days, Lady Beverley. I hope you will excuse my tardy arrival. I will explain the circumstances presently."

Araminta slithered into the room at that moment. Mr. Desford eyed her with suspicion. Cecil hurried to introduce her to the solicitor.

Mr. Desford stood behind the desk and took a moment to gather his thoughts. "I shall come straight to the point as I am sure you wish. At this time I would ask that the accountant – who is the accountant?"

"I am standing in for him, sir," responded Henry, stepping forward.

"Yes," he continued, "and, of course, Lady Beverley, Mr. Cecil Busslingthorpe, and Mrs. Mabel Jackson should remain in the room. I respectfully request that all other parties leave us."

"But, my mother . . ." Cecil began.

Mr. Desford held up his hand. "I am the solicitor here, sir."

Mr. Hydemark and Araminta started toward the door.

Bevie spoke up immediately. "Mr. Desford, I must insist that Mr. Hydemark remain in the room since he has been acting as my protector since my father's death. I would have thought it necessary that you would have appointed someone to oversee the affairs of the estate immediately. Is that not so?"

"Yes, of course, forgive me."

Mr. Hydemark slipped back into the room and closed the door, leaving Araminta alone in the hall.

"Pardon me," Henry interrupted, "I shall endeavor to find Mrs. Jackson."

The five gathered in front of the desk. "Please sit down, everyone," Mr. Desford began. "You are no doubt in suspense as to the reason for the delayed reading of the will. The fact is, not long before his death, Lord Burnside made out a codicil to his will. Unfortunately, those in my office have misplaced the document."

There followed a unified drawing in of breath and the exhaling of "oohhs."

"Now," he continued, "Thomas – that is Lord Burnside – insisted that he have a copy for his files and that is what I am hoping to locate as a substitute until we can find the original."

"Can you tell us the gist of the will?" Cecil asked impatiently.

"I can and I shall tell you the things that must be said at this time. However, I will not read the document in its entirety until the original codicil or a legal copy is located. This is merely an unsigned copy I have kept for my files."

"Just a minute, sir, this seems highly irregular to me. Why is it that things do not revert to the original will since you undoubtedly bungled the job?" Cecil accused the solicitor.

He glanced at Cecil with contempt. "It may eventually come to that, but please allow me to continue without interruption. Here are the facts that I will divulge. Firstly, Admiral Maximillian Kendall St. Ives has been appointed sole protector of Lady Beverley and is to have complete control of the vast estates until the distribution of assets is released."

Cecil interrupted again, "Here now, what about the heir?"

"I assume you believe you are to be the heir, Mr. Busslingthorpe?"

"I know I am."

"Yes, well it would appear that you are next in line for the title of Sixth Earl of Burnside. However, all of that will come to light at the final reading of the will. Another important reason for the delay is the fact that legal charges have been brought against the former accountant who has been accused of theft of property and monies belonging to the estate. Therefore, it is unlikely that any distribution of assets can be made until all of this is settled. That is not to mention that we sincerely hope to learn the identity of the murderer by the time the contents of the will are disclosed."

Lady Beverley found her voice at last. "This is all very unsatisfactory, Mr. Desford. How am I to know how to proceed and whether or not I shall find myself without a home? More importantly, who is this admiral you say is my protector? I have never heard of him and he certainly has not shown his face at a time when he might readily have been of some earthly use."

"From what I understand about the man, he was a close friend of your father while they were in Her Majesty's Service abroad and, I believe, he once saved your father's life. He is, as we speak, terminating his service in order to take up his position here."

"I cannot understand why my father would have done this."

"I am certain he had a very good reason. Now, that is all I have to say at the moment."

"Will you have a small nuncheon with us, sir?" inquired Mrs. Jackson.

"Thank you, but I must travel to my next appointment."

"May I have a private word with you before you leave?" Bevie asked.

"Certainly, if the rest of you will please excuse us."

As the others filed out of the room, Bevie moved to a chair across from Mr. Desford. "I have two pressing questions for you. Will you please tell me if Busslingthorpe is to inherit everything and if so, what would happen if I were to marry immediately?"

Alarm spread over the solicitor's face. "I thought you understood that until you reach – let me see here," he said as he thumbed through some papers, "yes, the age of five and twenty, you will need permission from your guardian to marry."

"What? That is preposterous. What if the admiral should happen to be a monster?"

Mr. Desford shrugged. "As to the properties, even the bank has a right to satisfy its losses brought about by the theft before any assets can be distributed. Surely you must understand the severity of the situation that was created when the man who had control of Burnside's estate manipulated the books and absconded with an indeterminate amount of money."

"I see that I am no better off than before you arrived, and possibly worse for the news that I have an unknown guardian. Can you not change things around and make Mr. Hydemark my protector?"

"I am afraid not, Lady Beverley. These things are written in stone and I am certain your father had your best interest in mind."

After a cold collation, the household scattered to their own musings. Cecil was becoming agitated beyond forbearance. "Let us walk toward the folly, Mother. I must speak with you where we are assured privacy."

"Walk, walk, walk. Walk again, Cecil? Why must you always require me to walk these vast distances? I am not young and my legs do not operate as they were used to do."

"Then come with me into the garden."

The two sauntered through the budding bushes and sat on a cold bench. Cecil leaned toward his mother.

"We must find the codicil and see if it will benefit us. If not, we shall destroy it."

"Oh my dear son, do you think me an idiot? I have had that in my head since you related to me the scant number of things the worthless solicitor revealed."

"It certainly is fortuitous that we are residents here. It reduces everything to a simple matter of searching for the document after the house has been locked up for the night."

"I hope so, but I do not believe the earl would have left it out in the open. Otherwise, it would surely have been discovered by that interfering Pick."

"Mayhap he did find it and did not like it. Mayhap everything comes to me!" Cecil squealed with delight at the thought, emphasizing his somewhat feminine motions.

"Who has a better right to search the house than you, my dear boy? You are the new Earl of Burnside. I am so proud of you."

An onlooker might have taken notice as to the slight enlargement of Cecil's frizzy-red head and the upward tilt of his thin, pointed nose at the mention of his new title.

"Trust me to make things right for you, Cecil. Your father failed you, but I shall not. You shall have what is due you."

Maximillian St. Ives, lately Marquess of Hampden, struggled to remove his driving coat and flung it at his gentleman's gentleman. "All these fashions are worthless. The uniform is the only answer. All men everywhere should be required to dress in the same uniform. I hope Burnside's chit is worth the trouble of this blasted journey. In all likelihood, she's an ugly brat who needs to be taught some basic manners. Why I ever agreed to this nonsense is beyond me. Did I mention whether or not Tommy wrote that she has a governess?"

"I'm sure I do not know, admiral, sir."

"What is her name?"

"I am not aware of it, sir."

"Liberty, wasn't it? A fitting name – I should like to give her the liberty to go and do as she pleases."

"Perhaps she will be quite agreeable, sir."

"Doubtful, very doubtful. I believe we shall rack up here for the night. The weather seems to be taking a turn. I'm in no hurry to get there at any rate."

"Yes, sir, I'll see to the bags."

"I shall enjoy my last night of freedom to the fullest. You must go and do the same since you may be thrown in with a household full of witless servants. I believe I shall arrange for a bonny meal and see if they have a card game in progress."

Pet and Nicky called at Burnside Manor the following evening and attempted to cheer Bevie. Mrs. Metterson set up a card table in the east saloon where Henry Pick joined them for a few games. Bevie could not enjoy it.

Pet was well aware of her friend's low mood. "Don't despair, darling. This Mr. St. Ives may be a reasonable man."

"Somehow I am inclined to think he is not."

Nicky took a turn at cheering her. "Come now, Bevie, you have nearly reached your majority, have you not? After that you may do as you please."

"Now there is the rub, Nicky. My father has left it that I must answer to St. Ives until I am five and twenty unless he approves a husband, at which time I will be free of his stricture and at liberty to do as I please. I believe I must try to gain my liberty by doing exactly that."

Nicky sank down in his chair, hoping she did not think him the best choice for matrimony. Bevie could not help noticing his discomfort and it brought a smile to her face.

"I was thinking of William. He has offered for me, you see."

Nicky sat up straight and sighed with relief.

"Please do not throw yourself into something you will regret," begged Pet. "At the very least, you must attempt to make a friend of St. Ives and perhaps he will do as you wish."

"Who wishes to make a friend of St. Ives?" inquired a deep voice from the doorway of the saloon where they sat.

Bevie gulped and knocked her chair over backward in the rush to stand up. She made a curtsey and said faintly, "Admiral St. Ives, I presume?"

"Indeed, and you must be Lady Liberty."

Pet began to laugh and could not stop. Soon Bevie joined in and before long the whole company was laughing.

"I see I am the brunt of your joke. Kindly allow me to join in," said Lord Hampden with a somber face.

"Please forgive me," said Bevie when she had gotten control. I am Lady Beverley." She proceeded to introduce the others.

"Lord Hampden at your service," he said, clicking his heels and bowing stiffly.

"Then. . . you are not. . .I thought you were. . ."

"St. Ives," he finished her sentence. "That I am. I have recently become known as Marquess of Hampden at the sad event of my father's passing."

"I am truly sorry," said Bevie. "Allow me to see that Mrs. Jackson prepares a room for you. Have you servants in tow, sir?"

"I bring one man and Mrs. Jackson has already seen to everything. When you are finished with your guests, I wonder if I might have a word."

Nicky and Henry Pick said at the same time that the game was finished. Pet declared that she needed her beauty rest. Henry thought she needed nothing to improve her beauty. Nicky went out to call for their carriage.

"Shall we have tea in the library, Lord Hampden?" Bevie asked politely after the group had dispersed.

"I sincerely hope Tommy stocked something stronger than tea. Brandy or port would be just the thing."

"Follow me, if you will. I believe you will find my father's cabinets stocked to your liking."

Bevie opened the cabinets and took out a glass. Lord Hampden poured himself a brandy and lifted his eyebrows, silently asking if she would care for a drink.

"I don't drink brandy, sir. Please be seated if you wish. I prefer to stand since I have been sitting all evening."

Lord Hampden blatantly stared at Bevie.

"Is something terribly wrong with me, sir?"

"How long must you wear those shades of mourning?"

"One year is customary, I believe. Why?"

"That color does not favor you."

"As to that, sir, the color you wear does not flatter you in the least and the waist coat is terribly out of fashion. And to be perfectly honest, that ridiculous spotted cravat – well, it seems to have been tied by someone who was . . . .foxed!"

"Contemptible little number, aren't you? I must admit that I expected someone who was still in the school room. Am I to understand that you have no governess? No, I suppose not," he answered his own question. "Then we shall just have to muddle along the best we can. Shall we call a truce? I promise not to condemn the color of your clothing and you may help me adjust to the rigors of private life and the awful fashions that are the current rage."

"I believe it would be a fair exchange, but first tell me why it took you so long to come."

"I came as soon as the news reached the port where I had been set down. Messages are not always delivered to a battleship in a timely fashion."

"Yes, I understand, but there are many things I wish to know about you. How did you come to know my father?" Bevie sat on the edge of the desk with her chin resting on her hand.

"It is a long story," he said, settling down into a comfortable chair and extending his long legs. His brown hair was curled around his collar as if he were unclear as to the fashionable length. His Hessian boots were rubbed to a mirror shine. His stature was slim, muscular, and fit. His ruddy complexion reflected many hours spent in the sun and salty air. His reflective brown eyes looked into the past as he spoke.

"I ran away from home as a boy. I was only thirteen when I had the notion to stow away on a naval vessel. My grandfather had often told tales of the sea, and after he died I was determined to experience everything he had. To make a long story short, Tommy – that is, your father – discovered me when we were far from shore and decided to take me under his wing. On one occasion when we were caught in a storm, a portion of the mast blew apart and I, having seen it, shoved Tommy out of the way before it flattened him onto the deck. It was the beginning of a lasting friendship, you see."

"Is that the occasion in which you saved his life?"

"So he said and then proceeded to inform everyone he met that he was my indentured slave forever." He laughed.

"It was a very brave thing for a boy to do."

"Posh, anyone would have done it. The thing is, you see, your father was a fine sailor and loved the sea. But, when your mother took ill, he left Her Majesty's Service to care for you and your mother. He loved his family far more than the sea."

A tear rolled down Bevie's cheek.

Max jumped up and put his arm around her to comfort her. "I am so sorry to have upset you. What a clodpoll I am."

She was so shocked that her tears turned into laughter.

"I do believe you have a soft spot in your heart, Lord Hampden," she said between hiccups and tears.

"Never tell a soul. I haven't the slightest idea how to properly react to a lady's tears."

"What will you do with me now? Do you know that Cecil Busslingthorpe claims to be the next Earl of

Burnside and intends to have the entire estate? I believe he will see me out the door the moment the will is read."

"Yes, Desford has informed me of the bizarre circumstances. However, I am most disturbed about the unsolved murder. Has any progress been made on the investigation?"

"I know very little about it. The police seem to enjoy keeping me in suspense. Mr. Hydemark, who has been acting as my protector in your absence," she emphasized, "believes that Constable Green wants to lay the blame at my door. I cannot fathom why he would think to do such a thing."

"I am beginning to understand that I have much to learn and even more to do in order to set things straight. Tomorrow I shall wait for you to tell me exactly what happened when you found your father, but let us now retire for the night. I am travel-weary. Bouncing around in a carriage is not the thing for me. I much prefer the rolling of a ship."

"Why did you leave the Navy?"

"It was fortunate that my ship had not left the port in England when news arrived of Tommy's untimely death. I did not wish to leave my ship in the midst of our country's concern with China, but I came to turn things right-side-up at Burnside Court, after which I must do the same at my family home in Yorkshire."

When Araminta was certain that Bevie and her newly discovered protector were ensconced in the library, she slithered along the wall in the darkened hallway to Bevie's rooms. First of all, she made certain that the maid, Suzie, was nowhere to be found. Then she proceeded to carefully wrap her Victoria handgun in one of Bevie's scented handkerchiefs that had been embroidered with the young lady's initials. She tucked it into the bottom drawer of Bevie's dresser, quickly rearranged the things she had disturbed, and hurried out of the room, removing her gloves as she walked briskly around the corner and down the corridor to her own room.

Her hand shook as she opened the door and she nearly jumped out of her skin when she felt a hand on her shoulder.

"Where have you been, Mother?"

"I am feeling restless and I was merely walking around the house in hopes that sleep would come more readily."

"What do you think of the latest arrival in the household?" Cecil asked, changing the subject.

"He may be trouble, but I am nearly certain that Constable Green believes Bevie killed her father. I think we shall try to help him along with his theory."

"I don't understand. Exactly what are we to do?"

"I will think about it and tell you tomorrow. I am very tired, Cecil. Go to bed, dear boy."

After Cecil left, Araminta collapsed onto the bed. The rigors of travel to her home where she collected her handgun, and the anxiety of placing it in a strategic location in Bevie's room, had begun to take its toll.

Before she fell into an exhausted sleep, she examined a few ways of alerting the authorities to the location of the handgun without insinuating that the detectives had been remiss in their previous search. Her one ally, Franklin, was perhaps the only avenue to such a plan. She would find some way to visit him in jail and promise him a lucrative position when Cecil was firmly entrenched at Burnside Court.

William was anxious to further his courtship with Bevie. He had dared to go into town and have the exclusive tailor, Gilbert and Drake, make him up the very latest in fashion and then assure the tailor he was authorized to charge it to his uncle. He was prepared for his uncle to oppose him.

Two days later his clothing was delivered. He practiced tying his cravat in the latest style for an hour before he gave up and summoned his uncle's man to help. He dared to ask him to attempt to arrange his hair after the fashion of the Corinthians. When he was ready, he slipped out the servant's entrance to avoid his uncle's discovery of his new and dashing clothes.

He arrived at Burnside Court expecting to be accosted by Busslingthorpe and his colorless mother as he was shown into the drawing room. To his surprise, it was empty of the annoying visitors. He stood and paced nervously as he waited for Bevie to appear. He was startled when a deep voice spoke from the doorway.

"I understand you seek an audience with my ward," said the handsome stranger.

William stuttered and groped for words. "I – I am – who might you be, sir – that is – she is your ward?"

"No need to kick up a fuss about it. Lady Beverley is my ward and, naturally, I am interested in acquainting myself with her friends and suitors."

"I did not know she had – pardon me, I am William Henderson, Lord Sedley's nephew. We, that is, Bevie and I, have been friends since childhood."

"I see, and that is the reason you are on such familiar terms with her?"

William blushed. "Yes, sir."

"May I inquire as to the reason for your visit today, Henderson?"

"Sir, if I may speak to you about. . . "

His words were cut short with the arrival of another person.

"Ah, come in, Hydemark. I suppose you know this fellow," said Max.

"Only since the – er – tragedy, Lord Hampden."

"He is on very good terms with my ward, I expect then?"

"As to that, I cannot say for certain. I know they have grown up as neighbors."

Bevie stood in the doorway listening. "Yes, we have roamed the acres together on many occasion, have we not, William?"

William found it difficult to put his words together. "I was – would you – I have my uncle's contraption and hoped we might ride along the avenue this afternoon, Bevie. That is, if I might have permission from Lord Hampden – and, of course, you as well, Mr. Hydemark," he quickly added. "Confound it, from whom shall I seek permission?" he asked in frustration.

"Why, Lady Beverley, of course," Max answered without skipping a beat. "The lady knows her own mind. Only she must, of course, have a chaperone. Will it be you or me Hydemark?"

Mr. Hydemark could not hide a smile. "Naturally, it would be you."

"Perhaps my maid should come along," Bevie suggested.

"No, I think not. I suspect she is too flighty," declared Max.

"How about Mrs. Metterson?" pleaded Bevie.

"She has gone out for the day," replied Hydemark.

"What kind of conveyance do you drive, Henderson?"

"A phaeton, sir."

"Then I shall come and attempt to hang on," Max announced. "Have no fear, Henderson, I shall be completely unobtrusive. You may act as though I am invisible."

"That is unlikely, sir, if I may say so," William said, totally put out by the turn of events.

Bevie, on the other hand, was delighted with the situation and saw a flicker of light at the end of a dark tunnel. *Perhaps my new protector will actually find a solution to my problems*, she dared to hope.

Araminta unpacked the clothing she had recently brought from home. She spread the housekeeper's uniform and a dark cloak out on the bed. It did not matter that it was wrinkled beyond hope. In fact, she believed it would add credibility to her mission.

She waited until the afternoon when the household generally lagged in activity before donning the outfit and walking quietly out the servant's entrance. She hurried through the gardens with the hood of her cloak pulled tightly around her head and took the path through the wooded area toward the road. She had no sooner reached the road when she saw a phaeton racing toward her. She nearly fell into the ditch in her attempt to remove herself from its path.

As it passed, she saw William driving with Bevie beside him and the latest arrival in the household hanging onto the back for dear life as the neighbor handled the horses in such a precarious way as to nearly land them in a heap.

She attempted to scrape the mud off her shoes in the grass and proceeded to walk the way she and William had come when she returned from home. She waited impatiently until she saw a hack coming along the road. She hailed it, but the driver ignored her and drove on thinking she was a maid with insufficient fare.

She struggled to walk nearly another mile before she was able to hire a hackney to take her to the prison gate. "Wait here," she ordered the driver.

"Pay me now. I don't want no escaped blokes strikin' me over the head."

Araminta started to walk away, but the driver moved the horses in front of her to block her way. She reluctantly paid him, hoping she had enough money left to bribe the guards to allow her to see Franklin. Being careful to keep her cloak covering her hair and most of her face, she approached the gate and asked to see her husband, Virgil Franklin.

"You won't get him out, woman. He done murder on Quality."

"He is as innocent as you are, I dare say – if not more so. You are Chenning, are you not? I have some information about you the police would like to know. Let me in."

The guard was silently sizing up Araminta's appearance and, indeed, concluded that word of his treachery might have spread through the servant's gossip line. "You better keep quiet if I let you in – not that I done anything."

Araminta gave him a look of contempt. He allowed her to pass by three guards to where Franklin was being held. In fact, she knew nothing at all about the guard save his name. She had paid a man to obtain that bit of information.

A broken and filthy man came to the barred door of the cage to see who was coming his way. Araminta handed him the basket of food she had stolen from the kitchen. He stuffed the food down before she could speak.

"I have come to help you, Franklin."

"Thank the saints, but who are you?"

"I am mother of the new Earl of Burnside. Remember?"

"Why do you want to help me?"

"Never mind that. I know something that will set you free."

"Go on, woman – speak your piece."

Araminta smiled as she walked past the guard and out of the gate. Her smile turned to a frown when she could not find a hackney for hire. Several rough-looking men stood about and shouted rude comments at her. She wished she had brought her handgun, but knew it could not serve its main purpose while she carried it in her reticule. She hurried along until she came to a tavern. A hackney was just coming along and stopped to allow a passenger to step out. She made haste to fly up into the conveyance before the driver could refuse her.

"Got the blunt, woman?"

"I can pay and there is no need to be so rude."

Mr. Hydemark decided to refresh his brain by walking down the avenue. He desperately tried to imagine where Burnside would have kept the codicil to the will. Since he and Pick had thoroughly searched the desk in the library, he was convinced it could not be there. He shuddered at the thought of removing every book in the earl's collection to see if the thing could be stuck inside or hidden behind one of the volumes.

Having exhausted this train of thought, he turned to go back toward the house. Just as he did so, he spotted a dark figure walking through the wooded area. Deliberately hastening his steps in that direction, he was forced to run in order to overtake the mysterious figure.

"Say," he said when he was within speaking distance, "who goes there? I believe you are trespassing on private property."

The person wearing a woman's black-hooded cloak shook her head and hurried along. He followed her into the servant's entrance of the house and refused to give up the chase. He dared to latch onto the string of the hood as she turned toward the back staircase. The gesture caused the hood to drop down and he saw that it was Araminta Busslingthorpe.

"Unhand me you monster."

"Pardon, ma'am, but I was not able to recognize the figure slithering through the woods. Perhaps in the future you would be careful to announce your presence."

"Perhaps in the future you would tend to your own business," she retorted.

He let her pass without further confrontation. "Mighty havey-cavey business," he said to himself.

"Good heavens, Hydemark, why are your shoes caked with mud? You must send them downstairs to be cleaned properly," Pick said as Mr. Hydemark entered the library.

"I was chasing a phantom through the woods. Turned into the Busslingthorpe woman."

"I knew she was a strange one. What was she doing in the woods?"

"I would very much like to know, but she told me to mind my own business."

Henry Pick laughed. "She will soon understand that is one thing you will never do, eh, Hydemark?"

CHAPTER EIGHT

Bevie heard the arrival of a single horse. She pulled the curtain aside and looked down at the entrance to see Constable Green coming up the steps.

"He is here again," she said to Suzie who was shaking the wrinkles out of Bevie's silk shawl.

"Who is, miss?"

"That awful Constable Green."

Suzie threw down the shawl and looked frightened. "What shall we do, miss? Perhaps we should run away," she said tearfully.

"Why are you so frightened, Suzie? It is singularly my concern. He is coming to harass me."

"I know it, but I am terrible afraid for you. What if he says you done it and puts you in jail – or worse?" Suzie's crying turned into sobs.

"Perhaps you should go down to the kitchen and have a cup of tea if it upsets you so. I have many people here who are willing to help me prove my innocence. I feel quite special and not in the least worried. Mr. Hydemark is a jewel and Mr. Pick can put that brute in his place. The fact is that I now have my appointed protector,

Lord Hampden, as well. I will soon learn whether or not he is up to the task."

By the time Bevie had received the summons to appear in the drawing room, two more visitors had arrived. Pet and Nicky pulled her into the east saloon the minute Bevie set her slippered foot onto the bottom step.

"Listen carefully, Bev," Pet implored. "Nicky and I stood outside the drawing room and heard that bowl-faced policeman telling Mr. Hydemark that he had uncovered some new evidence and was here to search your rooms again. You must hear what Nicky has to say."

"Yes, love," Nicky said in his sometimes broken English. "My very big passion is to take you away from this country that is accuser of innocents. Come now without delay. I believe you must suffer great danger here. My carriage waits outside. Do not gather your belongings, but come now. Pet has enough for both of you."

Pet and Nicky tugged on her arm and she had nearly decided they had the right of it when Max came rushing through the hallway and nearly bowled them over. Pet made a quick curtsey and Nicky bowed and looked bewildered.

"Anything amiss, my dear ward?"

"They believe Green is here to take me to Newgate. Perhaps he is. Shall I bolt?"

Max smiled at the trio. "How wonderful to know you have such loyal friends, Bevie. It is not everyone who is so fortunate. I am most grateful to both of you for your continued help in this matter. However, I wish to put your minds at ease. Rest assured I shall handle the matter without delay."

"But. . .he said he has evidence. What could it be?" Pet questioned.

"Who knows? The fool is no doubt at wit's end. I would suggest that the three of you proceed to the breakfast room and leave the greenhorn to me."

They all felt compelled to comply.

When they reached the breakfast room, Pet let out a sigh and whispered to Bevie. "If you don't want him, darling, I believe I shall take him, although I feel certain my heart is hopelessly attached to your beautiful accountant. Max appears to be about thirty. I suppose he may be a little old for you, but age differences are easily overcome."

Bevie was quite used to Pet's outlandish statements and ignored most of them. "What if someone else has planted a weapon in my room?" she asked with a definite foreboding. "I think perhaps I should go away in that case."

Pet secured a promise from Nicky who had agreed, under duress, to whisk Bevie out of the country. But, now that he had once again encountered the forceful Lord Hampden, he felt uneasy about doing anything that might incur the gentleman's wrath. "Are you sure? I think your man will help you."

"I do indeed hope so."

Max casually ambled into the drawing room.

"Where is Lady Beverley? I don't have time to wait for this household to leisurely sip their tea," Constable Green snarled with his lips curled and his teeth bared.

"What is it you want with her this time, Green? I am led to believe that your intrusions are becoming tiresome to the entire household."

"I have come with a search warrant and intend to search her room," he said, walking toward the door where Max deliberately blocked his exit.

"What do you hope to find there?"

"I know who you are, St. Ives, but I have work to do. Be so kind as to step aside."

"Perhaps you do not know who I am, constable. Marquess of Hampden," he said, holding out his hand as if to greet the man.

"I thought you were St. Ives," Green replied, stopping to quickly shake his hand. "What business do you have here and where is the suspect? My business is with her."

"I realize you are on a tear in your effort to convict someone of the crime, Green, but you are barking up the wrong tree if you think you will pin it on my ward."

"So you are St. Ives."

"Marquess of Hampden, as I said."

With that, Constable Green pushed his way past Max and trotted up the steps two at a time, opening doors and trying to remember where Bevie's rooms were located. Max followed closely on his heels and offered no help. Green soon recognized the rooms from the previous search and went directly to the dresser where the prisoner, Franklin, had told him he would find the handgun. Wasting no time, he shuffled around in the bottom drawer and removed the neatly wrapped weapon.

Max tried to hide his surprise. "Who told you about that?" he questioned.

"Afraid I can't discuss police business with you, Lord Hampden, and ever so certain I shall be calling again to escort your little lady to the clinker. We only lack proof that the bullet matches the gun, but I shall soon have it."

Constable Green trotted back down the steps and out the door with a look of triumph on his face. Max cringed. He went directly to find Mr. Hydemark and Henry Pick in the library where Pick was sitting behind the huge desk as was his habit.

"Where's Hydemark?"

"He had a few things to do this morning. Should be here any time, I imagine."

"We've got trouble and I could use some help from both of you. It seems Green has gotten a tip and stormed into Bevie's rooms where he directly located a neat-looking handgun – a Victoria, I believe. Do you have any idea whether or not Bevie owned such a thing?"

"She clearly stated that she has never owned or fired a gun of any sort. I can't be sure of it, certainly, but the more I know her, the more likely I am to believe it."

"Just so – as do I. Does it not seem strange that two different guns were found in her room and the second one was not found during the first search?"

"It's a sad business. There is someone who is determined to see Lady Beverley hung from the gallows."

"Tell me everything you know of those who could possibly desire such a thing, Pick. I cannot conceive of such a monster."

Araminta Busslingthorpe pulled the curtain aside and smiled with satisfaction as she watched Constable Green carefully tuck her handgun into the pack on his horse and ride off. She decided to allow things to take their natural course and refrain from enlightening her son. *It will be better if he is dumbfounded when he hears the news.*

Cecil was preparing for another long and boring day as he combed his curly, red hair and brushed the generously padded shoulders of his morning jacket. He made a decision. He would not pass another night without entertainment and purposed to ride into town before the evening meal. He was beginning to lose patience with the entire situation and sometimes wished his interfering mother to Jericho.

Araminta was overjoyed at the prospect of seeing the final blow levied on the uppity Lady Beverley. She primped before the looking glass and prepared to go downstairs where she could watch the unraveling of the household. As she passed through the long hallway, she collided with Mr. Hydemark who had just arrived.

"Good morning, Mrs. Busslingthorpe. I am quite at a loss as to what might be keeping you at Burnside Court. I was under the distinct impression that you had decided to leave after I encountered you slinking through the woods."

"Now what would cause you to imagine that I would leave the home that will soon be my permanent residence, sir? I have no intention of leaving."

"Forgive me if I have misunderstood the circumstances."

"Yes, I am certain you have. My Cecil will undoubtedly take over this household without delay and, should you be in question about the matter, sir, you will no longer be welcomed here after that joyous transition takes place."

"Oh indeed, I am sure that will be the case – if it ever takes place," Hydemark replied and then turned and walked away.

Araminta stood still, staring at his back, and wondering why he seemed so dastardly sure of himself. She could not abide the man's presence. "What has he discovered?" she mumbled to herself.

When Mr. Hydemark entered the library, he found Max and Henry Pick searching among the many volumes of books. "Looking for the codicil?" he inquired.

"Put on your gloves and give us a hand, Hydemark," said Max from the ladder.

"What makes you think Burnside was such a mince-brain? He would never hide the codicil in his bookshelf."

Henry and Max stopped what they were doing and looked inquiringly at him.

Max cocked his head to one side. "Well then, where?"

"Suppose you leave the books a little disheveled and entice the visitors to spend time looking through every one of the hundreds of volumes. That should occupy them for a time until we discover the true hiding place."

"Why wouldn't we find it in here?" Pick asked.

"It is altogether too obvious. It is the favorite hiding place in all of the current mystery novels. Burnside was astute. He would have thought of an unlikely place – that is, if he intended to hide it at all, which I seriously doubt. He naturally assumed that his solicitor would not be so foolish as to lose the original."

Max stepped down from the ladder and started to put it back where he found it.

"Leave it there. Our guests will want to use it for their clandestine search in the wee hours of the morning."

"Green was here and extracted another gun from Bevie's room," Henry announced, quickly gaining Hydemark's attention.

"I saw him on the road and thought he was up to no good. What kind of a gun did he find this time?"

Henry looked to Max for the answer.

"It was a neat little Victoria handgun, wrapped up in one of Bevie's handkerchiefs, and neatly placed in her dresser drawer. Green went right to it as if someone had laid out a map for him."

"In that case, I am certain someone has done exactly that," remarked Hydemark. "We shall have to discover who and why. I fear time may be running out and we must take drastic measures to protect Lady Beverley."

"Very true, but what is to be done?" Henry asked.

Max sighed and shook his head in disbelief. "It does look as though they will have enough evidence to point the finger at Bevie if the bullet matches the gun. No doubt that bulldog Green will delight in seeing the lady thrown behind bars. I believe I must take some precaution against it. I shall have to leave you for one or two days. Because of the likelihood that Green will come to arrest her, I think it necessary that we send Bevie into hiding with her friends until I return."

Hydemark objected. "I fear that will put her in a bad light if the thing should come to trial."

Max lifted his eyebrows in question. "What else is to be done? I cannot believe you wish to visit her in gaol."

"No, of course not. Green has something against her and will not see it any other way, I am certain. Very well, we shall take the chance that it will not do more harm than good," Mr. Hydemark agreed.

Bevie accompanied Pet and Nicky to the front door. As they were getting ready to leave, Max intercepted them and summoned all three to the library.

"We have a tenuous situation at hand. I know that I declined your offer to remove Bevie from the house, Mr. Gabrieli, but I have changed my mind."

Bevie was alarmed. "What has happened to change your mind, Lord Hampden?"

"Green has uncovered another gun in your room."

Bevie cried out. "No, I cannot understand it! Who owns the gun?"

"If I could answer that question, it would no doubt lead to the conclusion of this investigation. However, I have no confidence in this persistent constable and I fear he would delight in mounting up evidence against you, Bevie. In that light, I am asking that you go with your two friends and stay hidden until I send a message to their residence asking you to return."

"We shall leave for the Continent immediately," announced Nicky.

"No need for it yet, my friend. I shall inform you if it comes to that."

"In that case, Nicky, you will allow us to stay on your boat which is docked on the river," Pet exclaimed as if it would be a holiday. "Perhaps you might visit us on *The Rosa* while we are there, Mr. Pick," she cooed as she smiled up at Henry.

"That would be much the same as sending the constable word of Bevie's location," Pick quickly responded.

Pet pushed out her lower lip and pouted. "But it would be very enjoyable."

"No doubt, no doubt," said Hydemark distractedly. Nevertheless, I must advise you to take the ladies to the boat one at a time. They must dress alike as if they are one and the same person. Once you are both situated, be certain that only one of you is seen on deck at any one time."

"A splendid idea," chimed in Max. "Tell us where I may find *The Rosa* when I return from my short journey."

Some details were discussed and Hydemark attempted to hurry them out of the room. "Make haste and be off now."

Bevie's feet seemed glued to the floor. "What is to be done about Suzie?"

Max sighed. "That is a very good question. I shall ask Mrs. Metterson to distract her in the kitchen for the next quarter-hour. Bevie, I believe it would be best for you to change clothing with Pet and wear one of your lace caps to cover your hair as you leave through the front door. I shall arrange to bring Pet around to your townhouse on my way north."

Pet giggled. "It is all so clandestine. I feel as though I am on the stage."

Bevie was too distraught to comprehend her friend's lightheartedness.

It was well after midnight when Araminta met Cecil in the library.

"Look, Mother, I believe the accountant has been searching for the codicil. I hope he hasn't found it. Well, at the very least, he has left the ladder conveniently at hand. I shall do the climbing and you search the bottom shelves."

"Thank you, dear boy. I know we shall have success. I only worry that someone might see the lights in here and question our actions."

"Even if that should happen, there is nothing they can do. All of this will soon belong to us."

"Yes, son, does it not bring a flutter of excitement to   your   heart?"

"I am getting overanxious to have it done. Have you learned why Constable Green was here earlier?"

"All I can say is that he seems to have found more evidence in the lady's room. No doubt she did it and is becoming more careless as time passes."

"Do you think so? I tend to think it was that useless butler who did the evil deed. No matter, it will be to our great advantage if they believe the chit did it."

"It will relieve us of a great deal of trouble."

Fortunately, Nicky was able to sweep Bevie into his borrowed phaeton and rush her to his townhouse looking altogether the same as his sister looked when they left his home earlier that day. Although it was not quite the thing for the two young people to be alone in the house with only the few servants who spoke very little English and answered to Nicky's Italian instructions, Bevie felt relaxed and Nicky managed to entertain her with some stories of his wasted youth.

He was particularly animated as he recalled his past and slipped back into broken English mixed with

Italian. "I have the idea if they capture you, it is only that you tell them you were kidnapped by a handsome Italian Count who takes you away to marry him."

Bevie laughed. "I have a suspicion they would believe it of you, Nicky. How many young ladies have you tried to run off with?"

"No more than five. That is, five who were not willing to come with me. The one had a very big brother who did the fight on me."

"Do you mean he beat you?"

"He tried to kill me, but I am running to the cliff and jumping into the water. He could not swim."

By the time Pet came rushing into the house, Bevie was nearly doubled over laughing."

"What is going on here, darlings? Have I missed the party? Oh my, we must continue this little amusement on the boat."

"Do not call *The Rosa* a boat, Petra. It is a ship."

"Yes, of course it is, Nicky."

Bevie looked expectantly toward the doorway. "Where is my. . .er, Lord Hampden?"

"Your lord is on his way to find a way to save you, Bevie. I believe we must make this whole thing into a theater production when it is over. Think how exciting it would be. I could be. . . oh dear, never mind that. We must prepare to leave for the boat – that is the ship – the moment it is dark. We will wear cloaks. I have two, and although one is black and the other a very deep green, no one will know the difference after dark. I think it is best if Nicky takes you first and I will follow you later."

"You will certainly not travel alone after dark, Pet."

"I suppose that may be dangerous. Then I shall go before you in the daylight and you will come with Nicky after the sun sets. Remember to keep your hair covered since mine is so much darker than yours, darling. Oh, how I wish my beautiful accountant could come with us."

Pet's beautiful accountant was at that moment attempting to walk unseen along the hallway where the late Lord Burnside's bed chamber was located. Since his room was in a separate wing of the house, he was not familiar with the layout. He heard a scuffling at the end of the hallway and ducked behind an armoire. A maid came down the stairs from the servants' quarters and continued down another flight of steps.

Henry slowly opened doors, peering into the rooms. Most of them contained furniture that had been covered with Holland covers and were obviously not in use. He finally hit pay dirt in a room near the middle of the hallway. He quickly entered and quietly closed the door.

It was an enormous apartment with two separate sitting areas. A door led to a chamber containing a high, carved oak bed, several tables, chairs, and gas lamps. The heavy brocade window hangings were of recent vintage and the Oriental rug was obviously authentic. Henry sat down in one of the chairs to contemplate his task.

It seemed to him as though the police had been careless in their previous search and had left drawers opened and clothes lying on the floor. He wondered at the inefficiency of the maids who disregarded such a clutter. A moment later, he decided that Green had ordered them to stay away from the room. His next thought was that someone had recently been searching for the codicil and left in a hurry.

It was unlikely that Green and his henchmen were aware of, or had much interest in the missing document, but had concentrated on finding the murder weapon. Henry decided to look in the places they had already searched as well as some they had obviously overlooked.

He began with the small desk in the sitting area. It was filled with writing supplies and books of little interest to Henry. He moved on to an armoire and carefully lifted out the things that had not previously been removed from the drawers. Then he removed the drawers. As he was moving toward the bed chamber, he saw the knob on the door turn and his heart seemed to jump up into his throat. He stood motionless.

"Ahh, I should have known you would find your way here, Pick," whispered Mr. Hydemark.

"Frighten me to death, Hydemark."

"Should I have blown the trumpet and announced my arrival?"

"Oh, cut line and help me search. This place is a veritable disaster. I suppose Green's men have left it so."

Mr. Hydemark took up the work and spoke as he lifted the feather bed and poked his arm as far under it as he could reach. "I very much doubt that they did. I would think our most honored guests, the Busslingthorpes, have been here before us."

"Do you suppose they have found it?"

"There is no way to ascertain the answer to that question unless they come forward with the document. In the meantime, we should assume they did not locate it. We must work quickly since it would be quite uncomfortable to be questioned by anyone in the household as to what we are doing here."

Less than ten minutes had passed when Henry Pick, having excellent auditory senses, thought he heard a disturbance on the lower level. "Listen, Hydemark, I believe someone has arrived."

"I do hope it is Hampden. Exactly where did he go?"

"It was not for me to question him. However, I believe we must leave before we are discovered in here. I fear I heard the annoying voice of Constable Green."

"Would that I had your acute hearing, Pick. Let us hurry down the back stairs. I believe you are correct."

CHAPTER NINE

"Bring her to me this moment or I will search the premises until she is found," shouted Constable Green.

Cecil became extremely contrite and begged his forgiveness, although he was at a loss as to the reason he felt compelled to do so.

Mr. Hydemark and Henry Pick stood outside the drawing room listening to the exchange from a hidden position. "That toad-eating fool," Hydemark whispered to Pick concerning Cecil.

"Where is she? I command you to find her," continued the raging Green.

"I beg you to believe that I do not know, Constable Green, sir. I can only say that on occasion I have seen her coming home after enjoying a late night in the company of her friends. Perhaps she has gone out on a social visit. Women often do, you see."

The incensed Green could hardly control his temper long enough to keep from throwing things across the room. "She was ordered to stay in this house! I will see her locked up. Summon her maid."

"Yes, sir. . .immediately, sir."

Mr. Hydemark pulled Pick down the hallway before they were discovered eavesdropping. "Quickly, Pick, sit in your infernal position behind the desk in the library. I shall endeavor to disappear before Green sees me. Tell him nothing and anything."

"What does that mean?"

"Tell him she has. . . I don't know."

Mr. Hydemark had only just slipped through the French doors of the library onto the terrace when Green burst into the library quite prepared to draw blood. "Find that chit now before I throw the lot of you in jail!" he shouted at Pick.

"'Pon my soul, sir, I believe you are overwrought," Pick said with tongue-in-cheek. "Won't you be seated?"

"Shut up, Stick or Tick or whoever you are."

"If you wish."

"Tell me where she is," he demanded.

"You just told me to shut. . ."

"I know, I know. Where is she?"

"I believe she has left the house, but I am not privy to the actions of the members of the household. I am, after all, only a bean counter, as you so aptly and most recently pointed out. I am not first in command."

"Very clever, Tick. Where did she go?"

"Well, sir, I can only say that I saw her leave earlier and she was holding her jaw like this," he demonstrated theatrically. "Perhaps it was a severe toothache."

"I told that bird-faced redtop to summon her abigail. She certainly must be aware of her hiding place. The chit was under strict orders to stay in this house. Do you understand?"

"Oh, I do, but I suppose that if one has a terrible toothache, it would seem expedient to see a dentist in order to gain relief from the pain."

"Shut up!"

"So you previously ordered and then rescinded the command."

"I have a mind to arrest you as well as that interfering excuse for a detective. Where is he?"

"Unless I miss my guess, I suppose you mean the very astute and, I might add, very successful, Mr. Hydemark."

"Yes, of course I do, you fool."

"As to that, he has gone out."

"Where did he go?"

"Forgive me for asking, but just exactly who and what are you investigating? If Mr. Hydemark or I are suspects in some crime, would it not be proper to inform us of such a thing?"

"Oh shut up, Tick."

"Your vocabulary seems rather limited today, Green. I have heard it said that the mind is the first to go."

"If I weren't on the force I'd plant you a facer, Tick."

"Tut, tut, Constable. I believe you should try to calm down before you are the victim of a seizure."

"Yes, you are probably correct. I don't know why I waste my time on such a band of nodcocks. Is St. Ives gone as well?"

"If you refer to Lord Hampden, the answer is yes."

"Where has he gone?"

"I must repeat my former statement in that. . ."

"Just shut up, Tick."

Henry couldn't help smiling. Constable Green turned on his heels and went into the hallway. He turned back and asked, "What is the maid's name?"

"I believe you will find the answer to that question by engaging in polite conversation with Mrs. Metterson, but I must warn you that she is not one to be bandied about by bullies."

"Who? Oh, never mind. Just shut up."

To further his frustration, Green was met in the hallway by Cecil who said he had searched everywhere and was not able to locate the maid.

Green rolled his eyes toward heaven. "Just tell me her name. That is all I ask. Have I asked so much from you? What are all of you trying to do to me?"

"Sir, are you not well? Perhaps I should call for a glass of brandy."

"Just shut up!" Constable Green shouted as he walked hurriedly out the door, mounted his horse, and rode away.

Suzie came from the kitchen to find Mr. Hydemark. She was very concerned about Bevie since she had been searching for her since early morning. She very cautiously tapped on the library door and was told to enter. Having been informed that Mr. Hydemark was not in the house at present, she ventured to ask Mr. Pick if he had seen Bevie.

"I can only say that you need not worry about her."

"Has she gone away?"

"I am afraid I cannot exactly say, Suzie. Where is Mrs. Metterson?"

"In the kitchen, sir."

"Would you kindly ask her to step into the library?"

Suzie left the library feeling extremely confused and a little frightened. She could sense that something unsettling was happening, but she did not understand the workings of the people who had overtaken the household. After she relayed the message to Mrs. Metterson, she found Mrs. Jackson resting in her room and quite satisfied to have Mrs. Metterson lifting the burden of running the household from her shoulders.

"Lady Beverley is fine, Suzie. You seem very anxious and I think it is time you had a day or two at your leisure. Would you enjoy that, my dear?"

"Oh, Mrs. Jackson, that would be wonderful. I could see me da and me sis if I could be gone overnight."

"Yes, you must do just that, Suzie. On your way out, inform Mrs. Metterson that I have granted you some free time. There's a good girl. Have a nice time, dear."

Suzie was more confused than ever, but happy to have the freedom nonetheless.

"Do I hear music?" Bevie inquired of her companion.

Pet giggled. "Nicky has met the owner of *The Falcon*. That is the name of the boat docked next to us. The man is a musician and entertains his musical friends nearly every night. They play all sorts of music and he invites many others to come and dance or simply enjoy the tunes. Is it not wonderful? Oh, and the gentleman also told Nicky that he is acquainted with our mother and father."

"I hope he does not notice that you have a twin."

"He is too caught up in his profession to notice mere mortals. Oh dear, Bevie, I believe we do have visitors coming aboard. Duck into that closet over there, darling. We must not take unnecessary chances."

Bevie thought she would suffocate in the small space. She could hear voices above and nearly stepped out of her hiding place and gave herself up to the authorities, for she imagined they had found her.

In fact, at that moment two of Constable Green's best detectives were questioning Pet and Nicky. The constable had given them strict orders not to return without Lady Beverley Murray. "If I do not have her in custody within twenty-four hours, you will all be seeking new employment," he had warned.

"Tell us where you believe she is hiding," one of the constable's men had begged for some indication as to where they might look for the young woman.

Green had stomped around the room. "Try every dentist in the city. After that, you may visit every modiste within the country. Find her!"

Fully expecting to find the Duke of Struthers relaxing at his country estate, Max was dismayed to learn that the gentleman had repaired to his ducal seat. It was farther than he wished to travel while time was of the essence. Nevertheless, he was kindly offered a fresh horse and prepared for the long ride. The weather had taken a turn for the worse and he feared it would slow him down considerably. Once again he wondered what had possessed him to agree to take on the responsibility of a lovely young woman who had become helplessly entangled in a dangerous web.

It was unpardonable that he dared to foist himself on the duke's household at such a late hour, but he could only hope he did not offend his late father's best friend by being so bold. The butler yawned as he opened the door.

"Has your master retired?" he asked without preamble.

"Who is calling?" The butler yawned again.

"Pardon me. I am Lord Hampden, Maximillian St. Ives."

"Wait here, my lord. Lord Struthers has indeed retired for the night – as has the entire household," he added with contempt.

Max forgave the butler for his lack of manners. He removed his riding coat, laying it on a bench along with his riding crop and hat. He was exhausted and decided to sit on the bench to wait for the butler's return. He feared the butler was so tired that he would forget what he was doing.

Eventually the man came back to say that his lordship would see Max in his bedchamber. Max immediately decided it was not a good sign. He had hoped the duke would still be moving about or nursing some port in his library. He followed the butler and was ushered into a most surprising apartment that had been decorated entirely in bright stripes of red and gold.

"Come in, Max," said the older man who was propped up in bed. "What brings you here in this awful weather? It is not your mother, is it?"

"No, no, Lord Struthers. I do indeed apologize for my audacity. I would not have come if I had thought of any other way."

"Sit down, Max. You know you are always welcome here."

He rang for a servant who took a long time coming to his aide. She had obviously been awakened out of a deep sleep and forgot to curtsey. "See to a room for our guest and then bring refreshments for the lad."

The maid looked around the room for some indication that a child had arrived. Max could not help smiling when he remembered his early days when Lord Struthers had always referred to him as Alexander's fine lad.

"Now you haven't run away from home again, lad? No, certainly not. I see you are a man now. How may I assist you?"

Max poured out the long story of Burnside's murder and the unfortunate circumstances relating to his only daughter. Lord Struthers listened without interruption. When Max ended his sad tale, Lord Struthers plumped up his pillows and sat silently for such a long time that Max wondered if he had fallen asleep with his eyes open.

Just when Max was certain he had lost the man to slumber, he spoke. "Go to bed and get some sleep, Max. Tomorrow I shall return to the city with you. I'm ready to quit this deserted palace. It's the most boring situation one can imagine. Why, yesterday there were no visitors at all. I was happy to see you, my boy. I was beginning to believe the world had stopped. Go now and sleep. You look travel-worn."

Max bowed, thanked the gentleman, and was led to a comfortable chamber where he fell into an exhausted sleep having entrusted his problems to his late father's dearest friend.

Max was surprised to see the duke looking so spry and chipper the next morning. He had a bounce in his step and he seemed ten years younger than he had looked while he reclined on his pillows.

"The weather has turned in our favor, Max. I've called for my carriage. Let us get off to an early start. Do you imagine we can travel as far as London today?"

"It might be a very tiring journey for you, sir."

"Nonsense boy, I have done it for years. Don't you believe that I am ready to turn up my toes yet, young man. I have some fight left in me. By the way, Max, how is your mother?"

"I fear she is feeling very much alone. She declined my invitation to come to London after I left my ship. I do wish she would change her mind."

"Leave that to me as well, son. I shall have her dancing before she realizes it."

Max thought the man might just have the gumption to do it. He was a man of extraordinary persuasion.

Pet prayed that Bevie would not make a sound. Two of Green's detectives thought they had seen her leaving a hack and climbing aboard the boat. In fact, it was not Bevie, but since she and Pet were dressed alike, it was difficult to tell them apart from a distance which was, of course, part of the plan. Nicky confused the men with double-talk mingled with Italian. When they left, it was clear they did not believe a word he said. Nicky saw one of them hanging around the dock and knew it spelled trouble.

When Pet pulled Bevie out of the closet and told her what had happened, Bevie began to sink into the doldrums. She blamed herself for getting her friends involved in the deceit. She suffered under a burden of guilt concerning the whole mess.

An hour later, Nicky walked along the dock to be certain that Green's detectives had left the area. He was convinced they had gone.

Pet tucked Bevie into a soft bed in the cabin. "Nicky has gone over to *The Falcon*. That is the boat with the music, darling. You must understand that he is drawn to entertainment like a duck to water."

"You may go as well, if you wish, Pet. I shall be fine here. In fact, it may be a good thing for people to see you. In that way, everyone will assume there is only one of us."

"Are you certain you will not be afraid? I hate to leave you alone."

"The crew is here and I am very tired. I shall have a nice rest."

Pet held Bevie's hand. "Alright, darling, but I shan't stay long."

Bevie was truly weary. The gentle rocking of the boat lulled her to sleep almost immediately. She dreamed of floating on a cloud and bumping into other pillows of white fluff on which people she had known in the past were floating past her. On one of the clouds sat Lord Hampden with a trumpet in his hand. As his cloud drew near, he blew the trumpet to get her attention. Bevie awoke with a start.

Something seemed different. She listened carefully, thinking the return of Pet and Nicky had awakened her. She indeed heard voices and, in fact, heard sounds that were quite similar to a party on the deck above. At that moment, she realized the boat was moving!

"Oh dear. Petra Gabrieli, where are you?" she shouted as she jumped up and began to dress, remembering to pull the cap tightly over her hair. There was no answer and only the continued voices and laughing on the deck above.

She hesitated to go up the steps to survey the situation, but finally decided there was no other way of knowing why the skipper had chosen to sail. She cautiously stepped into the crowd and searched the faces of a gaggle of strangers in an attempt to find Nicky and Pet, but they were nowhere to be seen.

"Hello, my dear Miss Gabrieli," one of the guests said, laughing and taking sips from a bottle of strong drink. "How did you come aboard *Rosa* so quickly? I know I left you with your brother on *The Falcon.*"

Bevie quickly perceived that the man thought she was Pet and was convinced it was as well he should believe it. In that vein, she went along with the obviously foxed man and laughed the way she knew Pet would do.

She moved away from the amorous young man and edged toward the skipper's perch only to find that he had been replaced by a stranger. She quickly began to review her options. Although she was a good swimmer, it was cold and the water was at a dangerously low temperature. It was dark and she had no idea where they were except for the fact that they had not gone far enough to be on the open sea. She was very glad of that, but knew if they continued to move ahead far enough, they would indeed reach the sea.

One of the men burst out in song. He had a loud, obnoxious voice and sang a bawdy song of a sailor and his fair damsel. Soon others joined in and they began to sing and lift their glasses and bottles in a tribute to the sailor who was a sinner and left his damsel in the lurch.

The *refrain* continued.

"Oh, the sinner left, the maiden wept, and ho, now;

The man did sing, the bells did ring, and off he went to sea, now."

There it is again, thought Bevie. Everywhere I go I am reminded that we are all sinners. "Is that what all this terrible trial is about, God?" she asked in a loud voice.

"Ho there, Miss Gabrieli, talking to God are ye?"

The man was obviously in his cups, as was most of the crowd, but she asked him the question, nevertheless. "Do you believe we are all sinners, sir?"

"Now as for me, I am, luv, but my little lady is a saint." He laughed hilariously. "She says God will catch me one day. I wonder what He'll do. Send me down below, I suppose." The man stumbled away.

"Well, God, I hope you won't send me down below. I am beginning to see that I am truly a sinner like all the rest," Bevie mumbled as she looked down into the black water.

She felt it was hopeless to speak sense to the man at the helm. He was as intoxicated as the rest of them. She only wondered how they had managed to keep afloat and moving in one direction. For the first time since she had known her, Bevie was angry with Pet, wondering how she could have allowed such a thing to happen.

They had been moving along slowly for some time when a fog began to develop around them. Bevie became increasingly alarmed when she heard fog horns a short distance away. Thoughts of a collision and having to swim in the dark, cold water filled her mind.

Two of the men began shouting at the skipper to "move ashore and drop anchor." Several of them were arguing with him as they ran along toward the perch where he sat. When a small boat passed within extremely close proximity, one of the men knocked the man at the helm out of his seat and took control of the boat. He seemed to know something about sailing because he maneuvered the boat toward some flickering gas lights which Bevie hoped was a dock of some sort.

As they drew near the shore, Bevie could see other boats lined up in the harbor and she realized they would soon be dropping anchor. She hurried to her cabin and gathered the few things she had brought with her. It seemed very likely that the police would be involved in any incident concerning a runaway boat. She had to get away before someone recognized her.

Some of the men were beginning to shake their fuzzy heads and notice their circumstances. When the new skipper managed to bring the boat close to the dock, a scene like a stampeding herd of cattle ensued. The men were jumping ashore as if the devil were chasing after them. Bevie waited until the gap between the boat and the dock was minimal and followed the herd.

One of the young men offered to accompany her to her destination. Having no immediate plan, she accepted a ride in his hired hack. Her mind raced through a hundred scenarios such as going home, returning to Nicky's house, running as far away as possible, or turning herself over to the authorities.

"Would you be so kind as to ask the driver to stop at the Cotillion Hotel, sir?"

"It's not the thing for a lady to go into a hotel alone in the middle of the night, Miss Gabrieli. I fear your brother would call me out if I let you down there."

"Oh, no, my good sir. I shall likely call on my aunt who resides here. She will see that I am safe."

"Well, in that case, miss, I shall oblige."

There it is – another lie, thought Bevie, *and I have just begun to weave this tangled web.*

She entered the lobby and saw that the clerk at the front desk was dozing. She slipped past him and found a seating area where she plunked down in a chair facing away from the desk. It seemed as good a place as any to pass the night. She had her story ready if the man should question her.

She was just beginning to relax when the desk attendant stepped in front of her, studied her for a moment, and then asked if she would like a room.

"I – I saw you were very tired, sir, and decided to wait until you were awake to ask which room my aunt occupies. You see, I had planned to meet her here, but my carriage met with an accident and I am horribly late."

The man walked back toward the desk. "Step over here, miss. What is your aunt's name?"

"It – she goes by – her name is Dame Florence Rhys."

"There ain't nobody registered under that name."

"Perhaps she used the name of Mrs. Flemming."

The man looked at her askance. "Why would she do that?"

"Oh, she has just remarried." *Will the lies never end?*

"No Flemming here, lady. You got the wrong hotel. I'll call a hack for you."

"No, please, I fear she has also met with a delay. If you don't mind, I'll wait here until she arrives."

The man thumped his square chin. "Well, I'll allow you might be right, but I don't want no tramps hangin' about in the lobby. If she ain't here by morning, you find another hotel."

Bevie nodded and went back to her chair to wait for another idea to slip into her befuddled mind.

CHAPTER TEN

Mr. Hydemark flattened himself against the wall outside the bedchamber of the late Lord Burnside. He listened for sounds of unwanted company before he cautiously entered the room for the second time in as many days. He lit two of the gas lamps and sat down at the secretary. He prayed for wisdom to know how he should proceed. His thoughts turned toward the Scripture where he often experienced wisdom jumping off the pages into his inner being. He scanned the bookshelves for a Bible. "Surely any man of his stature would own a Bible," he mumbled to himself.

On his last turn around the large suite, he spotted a Bible on the table next to the bed. A ribbon marked a place. He turned to the page and saw that a passage had been underlined.

"The Lord is my light and my salvation. Whom shall I fear? The Lord is the strength of my life; of whom shall I be afraid?" Psalm 27:1 (KJV)

Mr. Hydemark studied the verse and became convinced that Lord Burnside had been a believer and was now enjoying heaven. It also seemed to Hydemark that Burnside was aware of the fact that he had an enemy.

He was in the process of returning the Bible to its place when an envelope fell out of the back and landed on the floor. Upon examining it, he found that it was the much sought-after copy of the codicil.

"Thank you, Lord," he said aloud, as he tucked the document into his inside coat pocket and extinguished the lamps.

"What are you thanking the Good Lord for this time, Hydemark?" asked a voice from the doorway.

"Be quiet and follow me to the library, Pick. I have something interesting to show you."

Bevie had fallen asleep in the hotel lobby with her head leaning on the arm of the chair. She awakened with a start when someone slammed a door. The sunlight shone through the windows reminding her that she had slept for several hours. She stood to straighten her wrinkled clothing and was met by an evil stare from the night desk clerk.

"Yer aunt ain't comin'. She likely weren't anyhows. Be off with you and find another place to sell your wares."

Bevie was shocked that he would insinuate such a thing. A sudden rage overtook her and she marched to the desk and wagged her finger in his face. "I sincerely hope you have another position waiting for you, mister, since you will not be sitting behind this desk much longer!" She arranged her cloak, picked up her reticule along with her small carrying case, and stormed out the door.

The clerk laughed at her back. "You ain't goin' very far, miss, if you get my meanin.'"

He was correct in that she had only walked a few steps when she was confronted by two detectives who had been alerted to her presence by the desk clerk. She was handled roughly and pushed into the back of a police wagon. At that moment she gave up the fight and surrendered to her fate.

Constable Green was anxiously awaiting her arrival at the constabulary. It was the first time she had ever seen him smile.

"I knew we'd get you sooner or later. You had your chance to get off with a lighter sentence, but now we'll see you hung. You caused us trouble, time, and manpower which throws me in high dudgeon when I consider it."

Bevie remained silent. She was somewhat relieved that her flight was over, but she dreaded what lay before her. She suspected that she deserved whatever it might be since she had recently come face-to-face with the fact that she was a liar and, yes, a sinner.

"What have you to say for yourself?" Green taunted. "We know you did it. Why not tell me why you thought we would not learn the truth?"

Bevie remained silent.

"Very well, put her in cell six," he ordered the clerk.

Bevie was pushed and shoved into a dark cell with only a cot to sit on. It smelled rotten and she cautiously sat down on the edge of the cot. She tried not to think about her future.

"She's a might pale, sir," one of the detectives later said to Constable Green.

"She deserves to be pale. Her father's pale as you can get."

"Yes, sir, but she is Quality. It could go bad for us if we treat her wrong."

"Leave that to me. Don't you have other work to do, Sergeant?"

"Yes, sir."

The detective acted as though he was leaving the building, but instead detoured to Bevie's cell and slipped her a cup of tea and a biscuit.

"Thank you very much," she responded. She had lost her appetite, but readily drank the tea. "I would not put you to any trouble. What did you say is your name?"

"Sergeant Pellman, miss. If I can help. . ."

"I know you are constrained, Sergeant, and I appreciate your thoughtfulness."

He nodded and turned to leave. She said faintly, "I hope you understand that I did not kill my father."

He continued to walk away.

It wasn't as though she did not feel like weeping, but only that she had shed all of her tears after her father died. She could not help wondering if he had gone to heaven. She felt certain that he was a good man, but then, Mr. Hydemark had told her that no one can get to heaven on his own merit. "It is only by the mercy of God and his Son who died for us," he had said.

It was hard for her to grasp such a concept. Why would an all-powerful Being allow His Son to be killed?

Her thoughts were interrupted by a matron who delivered some awful-looking gruel and a cup of black coffee. She took the tray and set it on the cot, thinking that she much preferred starvation to being hung.

A few minutes later, the matron returned and pushed her way into the tiny cell. "Who gave ye this?"

she asked, holding up the tea cup. "There'll be no more o' that."

She slammed out of the cell. Bevie had just enough pluck left to stick her tongue out at the hefty woman as she shuffled down the corridor to the next cell.

Her next visitor was none other than Green himself. "I thought I'd mention to you that Assize Court will be in session in two weeks. Supposed you'd want to prepare yourself for it."

"I believe I am entitled to representation, sir," she managed to say.

"If you think you can arrange it," he reluctantly agreed and quickly left before she could question him as to how she was to contact her solicitor.

"This is most interesting," said Mr. Hydemark. "It appears Lord Burnside had discovered that someone was attempting to trace his family tree and inquiring about the value of his estates."

"How do you know that?" questioned Pick.

"From the enclosed copy of the letter he wrote to his solicitor. It is also evident in the way the codicil has been carefully worded to make it foolproof."

"It still riles me to think that goon, Busslingthorpe, will inherit the title."

"It is a sad thing, to be sure. But think, Pick, he will not have two coins to rub together. I imagine his pushing mother will have an attack of the vapors when she learns the entire estate and every last asset belongs to Lady Beverley."

Lord Hampden was bouncing into London town, wishing the poorly-sprung carriage would transform into a ship. Lord Struthers sat across from him slipping alternately between a deep sleep and a restless snoring.

Suddenly, as if he hadn't slept at all, Lord Struthers announced, "We shall first go to the docks and locate the young man's boat whereby we shall retrieve your little lady, Max."

"Very good, sir. She is undoubtedly wondering what has become of me."

"Quite so – and then I believe it best if we confer with a barrister of my acquaintance."

"Certainly, sir."

Max knew better than to question the man who was one of the most respected Members of Parliament in England. When he spoke, people listened.

Max leaned out of the carriage and gave instructions to the driver. It was late afternoon when they reached the docks. Max jumped out and walked down the wharf looking for *The Rosa*. He walked back again wondering if he had the right name. He stopped to ask a sailor if he had seen such a boat.

"She were commandeered, gov."

"What exactly are you saying, man. It was not a warship   –   was   it?"

"No sir, but the word around is that some blokes went off with it."

"Have the police been notified?"

"That I could not say, gov. I only heard talk at the tavern."

Max thanked the man and walked back to the carriage to tell Lord Struthers the news.

"It certainly is an uncommon thing, Max. Perhaps we should go to the owner's home and inquire as to the nature of the theft. Have you any idea of his direction?"

"Yes, I once called at the residence."

"Then let us be off. Some havey-cavey business, eh?"

Max was becoming more and more anxious. Lord Struthers' driver poked along as if they were on a leisurely drive through Hyde Park. It took all of Max's constraint to keep from displacing the old driver and taking over the ribbons.

Lord Struthers sensed his discomfort, pounded his cane on the roof and shouted out the window. "Wake up and move these cattle along, Wardly!"

The pace picked up from that of a snail to a turtle. Lord Struthers mumbled, "I should pension off the old fool."

When they at last reached Nicky's townhouse, Max jumped down, lent a helping hand to Lord Struthers, and ran to the door where he impatiently banged the brass knocker.

Nicky met them in the hallway, quickly dispensing with introductions. "I suppose you have heard," he said, addressing Max.

"Yes, I have heard. Where are Bevie and your sister?"

"I thought you knew, my lord. Bevie has disappeared with the ship."

"What? How can that be? Why weren't you and your sister with her?"

"I am so sorry, Lord Hampden. I left my ship for only a short time to visit a neighboring boat and . . ."

"So you left her alone. What of the skipper? Where is the boat now? How could you two simpletons have done such a thing? You knew Bevie was in danger."

"I am indeed sorry, my lord."

"Who is the skipper of the boat?"

A tall, dark-haired man stepped into the vestibule where they stood. "I am the unfortunate skipper."

"How is it that you are not with your ship?"

"It is a long story. We were all invited to attend a musical on the neighboring boat and, whilst we were gone, some of the partiers boarded my ship and made off with it. Please understand, my lord, they were slightly intoxicated at the time and meant no harm."

"I am beginning to understand perfectly. You were all foxed and you allowed my ward to be kidnapped along with the boat. Have the police been notified?"

"Yes, my lord, and they have found the boat downstream."

"Good then, I shall find it and bring Bevie back."

"I am so sorry, Lord Hampden. No one was on the boat when the police located it."

Max turned white and then red. "Where is she?"

"I don't know, sir. Pet has been out looking for her since it happened."

Hydemark picked up his walking stick and hat. "I shall be gone for two days – three at the most, Pick. It may take me a little time to locate Mr. Styles' country estate. Very unusual for a solicitor to have a place in the country, wouldn't you say? Nevertheless, I shall find him and bring him back here to read the will. It is time these things were settled and we all got back to our places."

"Very good, Hydemark, but don't be gone long. I have a feeling things are not as they should be. I wonder why Hampden has not returned."

"That is a question I would answer if I knew of his destination. He is a secretive sort of chap, I surmise."

"He will be very pleased that you have found the codicil."

"Yes, and he will undoubtedly be happy to learn that his ward has been left with a means of independence. To realize one is responsible for a young lady of quality must be a great burden for a single man to bear."

Pick laughed. "I doubt it, Hydemark."

Mr. Hydemark shook his head and left the room. He encountered the ever-present Cecil Busslingthorpe on his way out the door.

"I see by the bag you carry that you are leaving, Hydemark. Has something happened to take you away from us?"

"Yes, Mr. Busslingthorpe, something has happened. Good day, sir." Mr. Hydemark tipped his hat and went outside to mount his horse.

"Stiff-necked buzzard," said Busslingthorpe. "I hope he stays away for good."

Pick had quietly come to the entryway. "Oh, fear not, Cecil, he shall return."

"Where has he gone?"

"I am not at liberty to say."

His attitude pushed Cecil over the edge into a fit of temper. "Why don't you go with him, Pick? I don't want you in my house."

"I am not at all certain the house belongs to you, Cecil. Why don't we wait for the solicitor to determine ownership? Let me absolutely assure you of one thing. If it is your home, I shall be the first one out the door. That is to say, I'll be just behind all the others who are rushing toward the exit."

Cecil turned angrily and went up the stairs. He burst into his mother's bedchamber. "I fear Hydemark has found the codicil, Mother."

Araminta shot out of her chair like a cannon. "Where is he?"

"He has just left the house to go – who knows where?"

"Well, don't stand there like a dunce. Go after him."

"Why should I do that?"

"If you weren't so dull, Cecil, you would know that he must have the document on his person. Go and stop him from delivering it. Go immediately."

"Well, Mrs. Busslingthorpe," he called her, as he always did when he was in a rip, "how shall I presume to do that?"

"Follow him, accost him on the road, knock him off his horse, or shoot him. I don't care how you do it, but you must stop him."

"Oh dash your fit, Mother. We don't know that he found the thing, and if he did, what it might represent – although. . ."

"Although what, Cecil?"

"He did say that something had happened."

"Where is that uppity girl?"

"I haven't seen her or her maid in some time. Likely she has bolted. Proves she did it, don't you see, Mother. She will hang and I shall inherit everything just as we planned. Rest easy. We only have to wait."

Araminta slid back down onto the cushion of her chair. "I wish you had more gumption, Cecil. You take after your father."

"You never did tell me how he came to fall over the cliff, Mother."

"Oh, go away and leave me alone."

The following day, William came courting only to find that Bevie was not at home. Henry Pick suggested that he return another day. After William left, Pick began to think it was odd that Hampden had been gone so long. He entertained the idea of going to the dock to check up on Bevie – with the notion that he would also see Pet, of course. After some thought, he decided it might draw attention to Bevie's hiding place and decided to wait for word from Lord Hampden.

He did not have long to wait. The commotion at the front of the house stirred the entire household. Lord Hampden stormed in demanding to see Mr. Hydemark, Mr. Pick, Mrs. Metterson, Mrs. Jackson, and Suzie in the library at once.

Given the man's mood, Henry Pick thought it prudent to avoid sitting behind the imposing desk as if he were in charge. Max's countenance was, at best, stormy. Henry Pick leaned against the mantle, Mrs. Metterson took a seat, removing her shoes to rest her feet, and Mrs. Jackson attempted to shrink into the background hoping to take refuge from the upcoming blow-down.

The room was silent except for the sound of Max's boots pacing back and forth in front of the doors that led to the terrace.

He suddenly turned toward Pick. "Where are the others?"

"Who?"

"Don't waste my time acting like a ninnyhammer, Pick. Where are Hydemark and that useless maid?"

"Mr. Hydemark has gone from the city and the maid, Suzie, as I understand it, has not returned from her allotted time off."

"Why has Hydemark left the city?"

"I prefer to explain the details in private, my lord."

Max paused and studied Pick's face. "Very well, then I shall begin. As all of you know, Lady Beverley was spirited off to a hiding place we thought most secure. As it happens, she was staying on Mr. Gabrieli's boat which was docked nearby on the river. Upon returning to the city, I have learned that the boat was commandeered by a bunch of drunken fools and Bevie – er – Lady Beverley is nowhere to be found. I had hoped to learn that she was sleeping peacefully in her bed, but the under-butler informed me that she has not returned to the house."

There were a few sighs and gasps.

"Just a moment before you speak again, Lord Hampden," said Mrs. Metterson who hurried to the library door in her stocking-feet and threw it open to find Cecil bending over and listening at the keyhole.

Max stomped to the door. "This is the outside of enough, Busslingthorpe. I want you and your sniveling mother out of this house by noon tomorrow."

Cecil straightened up and calmly said, "I shall not be forced to leave my own home, Hampden. You cannot order me to do so."

"Try me!"

Max slammed the door in his face and turned back to the small gathering. "When is her maid expected to return?" he asked, directing the question to Mrs. Jackson.

The housekeeper began to cry. "She was to have been back yesterday, my lord. I am so afraid something terrible has happened to Bevie."

"Yes, well that is the general concern, Mrs. Jackson. Is there anything any of you can tell me that might help me locate her?"

"Wouldn't Mr. and Miss Gabrieli be able to enlighten you, my lord?" inquired Mrs. Metterson.

Max's face turned red and he attempted to keep his temper under control. "That is what any sane person would expect, isn't it? However, the flighty Miss Gabrieli and her brother abandoned Lady Beverley in favor of entertainment on a neighboring boat. Therefore, no one knows where she went after she left the vessel."

"I believe we must begin by checking the hospitals," suggested Henry.

"That is an excellent suggestion. Begin immediately, Pick."

"Me, sir?"

"Who better than you, Pick? But, before you go, I would have a private word with you."

Mrs. Metterson stepped forward. "What about the skipper who stole the boat? Surely he would have seen her leave."

"It seems that he was one of the party of drinkers and was in no state to notice anything."

"Oh dear, this is worse than I thought."

"Just so. You may go about your business and keep your ears opened for clues. I shall question the rest of the staff presently. Pick, stay here a moment, if you will."

After the others had left, Pick explained that Mr. Hydemark had found the codicil and gone off to find the solicitor.

"What did it say?"

"The good thing is that Lady Beverley is to inherit the entire estate. The bad news is that the title will pass to next of kin, that being Busslingthorpe."

"I see. Yes, well all that property will not be of any use to her if we cannot locate her, Pick. Do your best to find her."

CHAPTER ELEVEN

"Might I have a cup of tea?" begged Bevie.

The matron laughed, showing her gums where three front teeth had once resided. "We don't serve no tea and crumpets in this 'ere 'otel. Fact is, we don't got to serve you nuthin."

"When may I contact my solicitor?"

"Ask the boss. How should I know?"

"Fine, then summon the boss and I shall ask him."

"Can't do that, missy. He ain't here," she chuckled.

Bevie felt dirty and was certain she was crawling with lice that inhabited the filthy place. She hadn't cried since the bars closed around her, but now she felt as though she would scream. She looked the matron over and decided that she had the propensity to be violent if any of her inmates gave her trouble. She sank back down on the edge of the cot.

The matron collected the tray, turned the key in the lock, and deliberately banged her keys on the metal bars for the duel purpose of establishing her authority and annoying her prisoner.

Bevie decided she needed to talk to someone. She called out to the other women in the block. They told her to shut up. She decided that God was the only one who was available. "I don't know exactly what I did to deserve this, God, but I suppose that I am a sinner. However, I do think this punishment is quite severe considering that I did not kill my father – or anyone for that matter. Now that I think of it, I must confess that I do wish to kill the matron."

Bevie waited for an answer. There was none. After a few moments, it did seem to her that all the unseemly things she had ever done went racing through her mind.

"Alright, God, I know I was unkind to William. Yes, and I am sorry that I lied so much. I know it was wrong to take the ribbons from the shop and I know I acted very haughtily toward some of the girls in the school. I do indeed confess that I am not a very good person. It seems that I have a very black heart, if the truth be known. In fact, I am sorry for all the things I have ever done and I am asking for Your forgiveness. Now, I know that You probably don't want to hear from me just because I am in a bad place and am now turning to You. I cannot blame You for that. I know it is not at all proper to be calling on You just because I am at my wit's end. But, there it is. Mr. Hydemark did tell me that You gave Your Son, Jesus Christ, to die for my sins and that You would forgive me if I asked. So – now I am asking. It looks as if I am going to die. I ask you to consider taking me to heaven. Amen."

Bevie listened for an answer. She wasn't sure, but she thought God did speak audibly to Mr. Hydemark since the man was always saying that God told him this and that. She had to admit that she felt as though a burden had lifted from her. She even thought God might have forgiven her – yes, she was sure He had. "Thank You for forgiving me."

It was during the night that Sergeant Pellman whispered to her from the outside of her cell. "Are you awake, miss? I've brought you some tea and a biscuit. How are you faring?"

"I am miserable, of course, but I am so thankful for your help."

"I wish I could do more. Is there something else I can bring to you?"

"Do you believe in God, Sergeant?"

"Yes, ma'am, I do."

"My friend, Mr. Hydemark, told me that God will forgive our sins if we ask. I believe He did forgive mine tonight – not that I killed anyone or anything like that, you see."

"We are all sinners."

"So you've heard that, too? That is very interesting. I keep hearing those words wherever I go."

There was a loud noise at the end of the corridor and Sergeant Pellman excused himself and hurried off.

A cold wind whipped around the corner tugging at the lining of her hood. Pet pulled her cloak tightly around her head as she stepped into the Cotillion Hotel. She had exhausted her list of places Bevie might have gone which were in close proximity to the dock where the police had found the boat. She approached the desk clerk and asked if Lady Beverley Murray had registered on the night of the boat incident.

The clerk hurriedly searched his books. "No Murray here."

"Thank you," she said, turning away.

The clerk stared at her. "Say, miss, warn't you here the t'other night? I seen you sit in that chair over there. You slept half the night. Said your aunt – well you told some woppin' taradiddle."

Pet jerked around and demanded to know more. "What happened to the girl who was here that night?"

"Thought it was you. Say, why should I tell you? She was a tramp and didn't belong in no decent hotel. This here is a fine place – or the likes of me wouldn't be here," he said, sniffing and tipping up his wide, pig-like nose. "I sent her out. Told the police."

"What? Did the police come and take her away?"

"Don't know – mind my business – ain't my job."

Pet wagged her finger in the man's face. "If I find that you have caused any harm to come to my dearest friend, sir, you had better run for your life."

"She your sister? She done the same shakin' her finger at me like that. I ain't afraid of either one o' you chits."

"Well, you should be. That lady is *le haute ton* and you, sir, are pig fodder!"

Pet stormed out of the building. She was so tired she could barely put one foot in front of the other. She had not slept or stopped looking for Bevie since the boat was stolen. She was devastated to realize that the entire thing was her fault. She should never have left Bevie alone on *The Rosa*.

She walked to the corner and nearly screamed when she saw that her hackney driver had left after she paid him to wait for her. She was almost in a state of collapse when a familiar voice called to her from a passing carriage.

"Ho, there, is that you, Miss Gabrieli?" Mr. Hydemark leaned out the window of Mr. Styles' carriage.

"Oh, bless you, Mr. Hydemark. Will you kindly take me up in your carriage? I have a need to speak with you."

Mr. Hydemark jumped out and assisted Pet, quickly making her known to Mr. Styles. "Please tell me how I may be of help to you, Miss Gabrieli."

Pet began to weep, but managed to get control of her emotions long enough to spill out the whole story to Mr. Hydemark and Mr. Styles. ". . .and the clerk said that he notified the police. I suspect they have taken her away, Mr. Hydemark." She began to cry again.

"There, there," he awkwardly tried to comfort her. We shall discover her whereabouts. I can well imagine that our slithering viper, Green, has her locked up somewhere. It is a Godsend that you are with us, Styles." Mr. Hydemark tapped his cane on the roof and gave the driver instructions to go directly to the constabulary."

Pet felt enormous relief now that Mr. Hydemark was in the forefront of the search. She knew Bevie trusted him and she had come to believe he was an exceptional gentleman. The carriage pulled up in front of the constabulary. Mr. Hydemark asked Pet to wait in the carriage.

"But, I should like to be the first to see my dear friend if that horrible man has locked her up."

"No, I think not, Miss Gabrieli. First of all, it is no place for a lady, and secondly, I believe that if Lady Beverley has been incarcerated here, she will not wish anyone to see her."

"Yes, of course, you are correct. It must be a frightful place." She shuddered.

Constable Green happened to be walking past the window when he saw Hydemark stepping out of a fine-looking carriage with an impressive crest on the side. He quickly donned his coat and hat and stepped out the back door.

Mr. Hydemark casually looked around for Green as he entered the building. He caught sight of him leaving by the back door. He stepped up to the clerk's desk. "Where has the coward gone?"

"Who, sir?"

"That cowardly boss of yours. Get me the key to Lady Beverley's cell. I have come to take her home."

"I aren't able to do that, sir. The only person who 'as the right is the constable 'imself."

"Don't practice your flummery on me, young man. Mr. Styles here is her solicitor and she has undoubtedly been denied counsel. That is a crime, sir, and I believe your reluctance will make you an accessory to the crime if you do not oblige me immediately."

The young man looked around for some help. He studied the face of Mr. Styles who was glaring at him. "Well, I 'aven't done it before, but I'll get the keys."

"Where is she?" Mr. Styles demanded when the young man handed him the key.

"She is in five or six."

"Lead the way, man," said Mr. Styles.

"Can't leave my post."

Mr. Styles went behind the desk and lifted the young man up by his collar. "I said lead the way."

"Yes, sir."

Suzie crept quietly into the servant's entrance, fearful of meeting Mrs. Jackson. She rehearsed a story she thought sounded plausible. Nobody in the house knew her relatives and if she told them her aunt had died, they would surely excuse her tardiness. She slipped into her room and put on her black dress, apron, and cap before tapping on Lady Beverley's door. When there was no answer, she slipped down to the kitchen. The cook looked at her with disdain and turned away.

"Where's my lady gone, Claude?"

"If you'd a been here, you'd a known."

"Well, I went to a funeral. I 'ad permission and 'er ladyship knows."

"She don't know it. She's gone missin'."

"Oh no, where did she go?"

"If you had anything in the brainbox, you'd a known that if yer missin' nobody knows where you went."

"Then where's 'er Lord Hampden?"

"Don't know."

"He's missing, too?"

"He's left."

"You don't know nuthin', Claude. I 'ave to see Mrs. Jackson."

"I hope she gives you a proper set-down."

She found Mrs. Jackson in her room pacing back and forth in front of her window. "I am sorry to be late, Mrs. Jackson. My aunt was awful sick and passed while I was 'ome."

"What? Oh – I am sorry, dear."

"I 'eard Lady Beverley is missin'."

Mrs. Jackson began to weep. "I just don't understand how this could have happened."

The conversation was abruptly interrupted when Mrs. Metterson came through the door that Suzie had left standing open. "Where have you been, Suzie? You were given the opportunity of having a day off and we expected you back the next evening."

"I am sorry, Mrs. Metterson," Suzie said, looking appropriately sad as she told the tale of her aunt's death.

Mrs. Metterson did not believe her. She had heard many stories from various servants and most of them involved a dying relative. "I want you to help the chambermaids today."

"But, ma'am, I am Lady Beverley's abigail. I was put upward."

"Well, I am putting you downward for a while. That is all, Suzie."

Suzie left the room thinking she should have run as far away from London as she could manage on the money she had saved. At the very least, she could have run to her sister's house in Brighton where she might have hidden from everyone.

"I do not understand why you promoted that girl to personal maid, Mrs. Jackson. There is something very wrong with her, you know." Mrs. Metterson said after Suzie was out of earshot.

"She was the only available maid I could trust and she is devoted to Bev – er – Lady Beverley. Oh, what has become of our dear girl, Mrs. Metterson?"

"Please sit down and stop that infernal pacing. It will all come around in the end."

"But, what of that protector of hers? He has done everything except what he is supposed to do – protect her. I am so afraid that someone has run off with her. She is such a beautiful girl and when I think of those awful men on that boat. . ."

"Now, listen to me, Mabel, you must pull yourself together. Lady Beverley has a good head on her shoulders. She will come through. And, if I may say so, Mr. Hydemark is a grand prayer warrior. He will call on God to bring her home."

"How can you be so sure? Is God at hand whenever Mr. Hydemark wants him? I think not, Mrs. Metterson."

"You may not think so, Mabel, but you are quite mistaken."

Max had given Henry Pick instructions to meet him at the four-story brick London townhouse of Lord Struthers where the gentleman was in conference with his friend and barrister, George Forsythe. Max was just approaching the footman at the front of the house when Henry Pick jumped out of a hired hack.

"Good timing, eh, sir?" remarked Henry.

"Quite so. Have you found any trace of her, Pick?"

"I regret to say that I have not. On the other hand, I am happy to say that I have not."

"It is no time to talk foolishly. What are you saying?"

"Well, sir, I checked every hospital in the area and no one there had seen her. That is good, isn't it?"

"I suppose it is," Max said as he handed his card to the butler.

"I was told to expect you, Lord Hampden. Follow me into the library, please," said the butler.

"Well, Max, I thought you'd never get here." Lord Struthers came to his feet as the men entered the room. "You know George Forsythe, and this is Mr. Pick, George."

Mr. Forsythe moved toward the door. "Gentlemen, I suggest we first make an appearance at the home of Lady Beverley and have a chat with some of the servants. Where is that fellow who has been hanging around waiting to become the next earl? I'd like to have a look at him as well. Sounds a bit off to me, if you understand my meaning," George snickered. "After that we shall toddle along to see what can be done about this fellow, Green. I suggest we all travel in my barouche – present a united front, you see."

Max had seen Forsythe's new carriage with the decorative gold trim. He smiled, knowing the barrister only wanted to show it off.

Mrs. Jackson was still pacing about the room when all of the servant's bells began to ring at once.

"Good heavens, Mabel, what has happened?" cried Mrs. Metterson as she hurried from the room followed by Mrs. Jackson. They nearly collided with a handful of servants rushing in the same direction toward the staircase.

Mrs. Metterson reached the library where Mr. Pick was directing everyone to the ballroom. "Lord Hampden has returned and wishes to have a word with everyone in the house," he informed each one as they came to the door of the library where the servants usually reported when several of the bells rang simultaneously.

When Mrs. Jackson and Mrs. Metterson arrived in the ballroom, Max asked them to be seated near him. "Do you know how many servants are in the house proper, Mrs. Jackson?"

"Yes, my lord, there are thirty-four all-told."

"Good heavens, why does one household need so many?"

"Lord Burnside hated to let anyone go, you see, even as some of us require a pension," she hinted.

He smiled knowingly.

The servants were standing nervously around the sides of the vast room when Max asked whether or not everyone was present.

"The outside servants, stable hands, and those who tend to the estate grounds are not here, my lord," Mrs. Jackson told him. She glanced around the room. "I do not see Lady Beverley's maid."

Max asked the general assembly if they knew where Suzie had gone. Cook made a remark about her hiding.

"I would like to introduce my dear friend, Lord Struthers, as well as his barrister, Mr. George Forsythe, who have come to help untangle the mystery we have here. They may wish to ask pointed questions and I ask that you answer simply and honestly." Max stepped back to allow the two men to take charge.

"First of all, I wish to have a word with the fellow who is to become the new earl," commanded Lord Struthers.

Mrs. Metterson stepped forward, and speaking to Max said, "Sir, if you recall, you asked him to leave the premises. He and his mother have gone but left word that they would return tomorrow."

"Very well," said Struthers. "Have we got the bunch here, then?"

"I shall attempt to find Lady Beverley's maid," offered Mrs. Metterson. "She was with me not five minutes ago."

When Suzie saw everyone running down the hallway, she became frightened and went out the servant's door to hide in the stables. Just as she arrived, William was leading his horse toward her.

"Fine day, Suzie. How does your lady do?"

"She's gone a-missin', sir."

"You can't mean it. How long has she been absent?"

"I don't know, sir. Them that's looking for her are together in the ballroom."

William ran to the house and into the front entrance that had been left unattended. He burst into the ballroom and stopped dead in his tracks when he saw the notable Lord Struthers holding forth in front of the entire household.

Lord Struthers paused momentarily before addressing William. "Well, I know this young upstart. What brings you here, Henderson?"

"Good day, sir. I have only this moment heard that my dear friend, Lady Beverley, is among the missing. I have come to help in any way I might."

"Yes, I begin to understand. Sit down and listen, son."

Lord Struthers looked toward the door. "I still await the arrival of the young lady's maid."

"I saw her in the stables, my lord," William remarked.

"Well, someone go and bring her here! William, the task must fall on you."

William reluctantly left the gathering. He had so wanted to hear whether or not Lord Struthers was discussing anything that might implicate him in the murder. He reached the stables and found only the stable boys who were brushing down the horses.

"Where did the maid go?" he asked Kit.

"I saw some cove on the path and he beckoned to her to come with him."

"One of the servants, was he?"

"No, sir, I don't think he was. The bloke had a cape over him so as I couldn't see his face."

"Which way did they go?"

"By way of the woods, sir, but they'd be over to the road long ago."

William reluctantly went back to join the group in the ballroom, taking with him the information Kit had given him.

The questioning was cut short by a commotion at the front of the house. Max insisted that everyone should remain while he went to the front. There he met the sorriest sight he had seen in many months. Mr. Pick was carrying a disheveled and dirty Bevie up the steps while Mr. Hydemark held Max back from going to her.

"Give her time to bathe and compose herself, Lord Hampden."

"Where on earth has she been to come home looking like a street urchin?"

"She has been locked in a cell, sir."

"Who has had the audacity to do this to her, Hydemark?"

"I suppose you know the answer to that. He slipped out the back door of the constabulary the moment he saw me coming."

"Green?"

"Yes."

"I'll have that man's head on the chopping block. How did all of this happen?"

"I believe I will allow Lady Beverley to explain. I heard it second-hand from her friend, Petra, who relentlessly pursued her until she was able to track her down. Now, here is an important thing you should know, Hampden. The authorities have definitely matched one of the bullets taken from Burnside to the handgun recently found in Bevie's room."

"That undoubtedly will make things very difficult for my ward."

"It most certainly shall. What is more, they have every reason to arrest her now and put her back in a cell. I can see this thing is bound for the courts."

CHAPTER TWELVE

William sat beside Bevie and nearly wept under the heavy burden of guilt he bore. He was torn between confessing that he had accidentally shot a bullet through the glass door and killed her father or finding some other way to exonerate Bevie. On top of that, he had planted his gun in the garden shed and further implicated Bevie in the death.

"If only I could stand in your place, my dear girl."

"I must face whatever comes to me, William, but I thank you for your concern. I should set your mind at ease on one point. In the event that they end my life, I am certain that I shall join my father in heaven. Mr. Hydemark has given me confirmation of my father's belief in Christ and I have faith as well, you see."

William nodded assent to her statement and fell silent as troubling thoughts raced through his mind. He decided to disclose his plans. "Listen carefully, Bev. I am going to kidnap you and remove you from the country."

"You are never serious, William. That is preposterous."

"It is the only answer. I have heard of others fleeing to the Continent and keeping safe from English prosecutors. We would be married, of course. I would not have it said that I compromised you in any way."

"I would not have told you, William, except that you propose such a cowardly way out, but there are others who have offered to spirit me off to far-away places in the world."

William thought immediately of Cecil. He saw him as his prime competition where Bevie – and her money – were concerned. "Am I to understand that Cecil and his mother will soon return to Burnside Court?"

"They mentioned their plans to return this day. I cannot be concerned about them. I have more important things on my mind. Lord Hampden and Lord Struthers are trying to arrange matters so that I may remain here instead of being kept in one of those horrid cells which, I think, must mock the circumstances of hell. I have been thinking about Franklin. Although I believe he was involved in the theft of my father's property, I cannot wish him to stay in gaol. It is not fit for rats."

"That is very big-hearted of you, Bev, but I believe the man is dangerous."

"Perhaps."

William was anxious to establish his plan. "I want to make it obvious that you were kidnapped so that no one can think you ran away, Bevie."

"I. . ."

Her reply was interrupted by Max. "There you are. I have been looking for you to tell you the news. Lord Struthers has arranged for you to stay in your home until the trial is over."

"Thank you, Lord Hampden. I believe death would be preferable to staying in one of those filthy cells. While you are here, I wish to ask you if there is some way you can arrange to free Franklin. I will admit to disliking the man, but I cannot live with the thought that anyone is incarcerated in those filthy conditions, no matter what the crime."

"Under the circumstances, there is no possible way to obtain his release until he stands trial, Bevie. It is, after all, what happens to people who steal from others. If he is innocent, he will go free. Now, Mr. Henderson, if you will excuse us, we have much to consider. Mr. George Forsythe has agreed to represent Bevie at the trial. He is the best by far. He will, of course, confer with Mr. Styles."

William excused himself and went on with his plans to kidnap Bevie. Max explained to Bevie that she would sit with Mr. Forsythe for at least an hour while he gathered all the facts needed for her defense.

At the outset of the meeting with the barrister, Bevie was in a daze and could not think properly. She asked for assistance from Mr. Hydemark who willingly sat beside her and held her hand to comfort her. He was also able to prompt her and fill in some details that had not yet come to Bevie's attention, such as the bullet hole in the glass doors and the footprints on the terrace.

It was during the intense meeting taking place in the library that Cecil and Araminta Busslingthorpe returned to Burnside Court and learned of Bevie's trial.

The gossip had been passed from the under-butler to the cook, who naturally told the upstairs maid, who did not at all favor Lady Beverley and made the fact known to Cecil, who had winked at her on one occasion when she supplied him with clean linens. This news only made Cecil and his mother laugh delightedly, being certain that the outcome would be a hanging, and therefore a veritable fortune for them.

Max and Lord Struthers conferred in Max's rooms where they would be out of earshot of the various members of the household. "I believe it would be to our advantage to speed up the trial, Max," Lord Struthers suggested.

"Why is that, sir?"

"Simply because of the evidence your people have uncovered which has been overlooked by the investigators – or so we must assume. The more time we allow to pass, the more likely they are to uncover some of it. I see it as ammunition for the defense."

"Quite so, Lord Struthers. Is it possible to change the calendar for the Assize?"

"It is a simple matter where the murder of a peer of the realm is concerned."

"Then let it be done, my lord, and thank you for coming to assist us."

Bevie was suffering from a state of mental exhaustion when Pet came to visit that evening. "How can I ever make it up to you for being such a fool and leaving you alone on *The Rosa*? Will you ever find it in your heart to forgive me, Bev? You are my dearest friend and you must know that I would never intentionally do anything to harm you."

"Please do not concern yourself about the matter, Pet. I will admit that I was, at first, very angry to find myself in such a fix, but it soon turned into my own folly. I should have simply turned myself over to the authorities and none of that would have taken place."

"It is not too late to leave the country with Nicky. Please listen to reason, darling. You must leave before the trial. It will be impossible to do so if they find you guilty."

"I have every intention of seeing this through to the end of the trial. I have become convinced that God will take care of me regardless of the outcome."

"But, we must be sensible. The courts are often wrong and the men do not know you as your friends do."

"Let it be, Pet, and pray for me if you will."

It was well after midnight when Bevie was awakened by a noise at her window. She knew at once what it was. She leaped out of bed and drew aside the hanging draperies. She couldn't help laughing when she saw William tottering on a ladder that was leaning against her window. He tried to open the window, but the ladder was heavily pressed against the panes, presenting him with the option of opening the window and falling off the ladder, or climbing down, moving the ladder over, and climbing up once again.

"Go away, William," Bevie said in a loud whisper. "I am not going to run away with you."

"Come, Bev, you must. Wait until I move the ladder. Bring a few things with you and a little of the blunt since I am not flush at the moment."

He gingerly backed down on the rungs of the ladder until he reached the ground where he promptly bumped into something that felt altogether like a person.

"Well, my good man, what is this?"

William nearly fainted with fright. He was speechless.

"Has the lady agreed to elope with you?"

"N – n – no, sir. I was just – I wanted to help – she should leave. . ."

"It is very noble of you to want to help, William, but it would be the worst possible thing, you see."

"How so, sir? They may decide to hang her."

"I do not believe they will, but it must be a matter of prayer. God is in control of these things. The outcome will depend upon His will."

"You sound so certain that she will not be found guilty. I offered to marry her."

"Did she agree?"

"No, but she doesn't know what is best for her. I am a man and I think it would be the most expedient thing."

"I see. Perhaps you also had a vague impression that you might become the recipient of any funds she might receive. Can you not see that if you took her off to – oh, say – America, she would lose anything that might otherwise come to her? What kind of existence would that be for the two of you?"

William felt defeated. "Yes, I suppose you are correct. Well then, what is to be done? Surely you are not going to stand by and see her hung or locked away for life."

"Lord Hampden has obtained the services of the best legal council available, and we must all pray."

"It does not seem to be enough. Suppose that it comes out. . . "

"Suppose what comes out?"

"Never mind, Mr. Hydemark, I have to believe you are right."

"Go home, William. You shall be informed of the outcome soon enough."

William left the ladder where it had fallen and slowly rode his horse home, taking the road rather than the path through the woods. As he was passing through the gates at the entrance, he saw the shadow of someone moving along the edge of the trees. He decided it was one of Green's detectives hired to make certain Bevie did not escape.

Cecil hadn't yet learned whether or not the codicil had been found since no final reading of the will had taken place. That night, he decided to give one last look among the bookshelves in the library. He was on the ladder and searching behind the volumes on the top shelf when he thought he heard a noise on the terrace. He turned down his lamp and quietly stepped down to the floor. He crept to the French doors and was ready to open them when something crashed down on his head. He crumbled to the floor.

Mr. Hydemark had just returned from his discussion with William beneath Bevie's window when he was certain he heard a commotion in the library. Thinking it was Henry in his usual habit of working late into the night, he made his way toward the library and found it dark. He lit the gas lamp and saw Cecil sprawled out on the floor near the French doors which had been left open.

Thinking the man had been the second victim of the murderer, he rushed over to make certain he was dead. Just as he bent over to check for a pulse, Cecil opened his eyes.

"Why did you hit me, Hydemark?"

"I certainly would never crack you on the head, Mr. Busslingthorpe, although I have often felt as though I might like to do so. Who was it that attacked you so viciously?"

"I don't know. I didn't see him."

"Perhaps you would enlighten me as to what you were doing in here in the middle of the night."

Cecil groaned and held his head. "Help me get up. I have every right to be wherever I choose. It will soon be my house."

Hydemark assisted Cecil to a chair and stood beside him. "Had you opened the doors?"

"I disremember. . .wait. . .I heard a noise and was just going to open them when someone came up behind me."

"It seems, then, that your attacker left through the glass doors. Would you be against my having a look at the bump on your head?"

"Go right ahead if you are certain you did not do the deed yourself."

"Don't be absurd, man. Do I seem like a violent person?" Mr. Hydemark pulled the gas light closer and examined the wound on Cecil's head. "It looks as though it was done with the blunt end of an instrument such as the butt of a gun. I must say you are fortunate your attacker did not choose to use the other end and pull the trigger or you may have been the second victim of a murderer."

"It is beginning to look as though there is someone out there who is determined to eliminate the Earls of Burnside," Cecil declared.

"You may be correct, but who could benefit from that?"

"That little twit, Beverley."

The morning of the trial found Bevie determined to go about her day as usual. One of the maids helped her dress in her mourning clothes after which she went to the breakfast room to have her usual chocolate drink and toast. Henry Pick greeted her and stood to pull out a chair for her.

"You seem in good spirits this morning, Bevie."

"I am trying to be calm."

"If it is of any interest to you, Hydemark has spent the last hour praying for you."

"He is a dear man."

"He is a man of great understanding."

Max stood in the doorway and interrupted their conversation. "Lord Struthers has arrived with his carriage, Bevie. It has been arranged that he will convey the two of us along with Mr. Forsythe." He turned to Henry. "I trust you will accompany Mrs. Metterson, Mrs. Jackson, and Mr. Hydemark in the Burnside carriage. Mr. Styles and Mr. Desford will meet us at old Bailey in the courtroom."

"How long before we must leave?" Bevie inquired.

"Lord Struthers feels that we should leave immediately, but it is equally important for you to have some nourishment, Bevie. So, finish up there and make yourself ready. I shall await you in the front."

Naturally, Bevie could not finish her toast. "This is it," she said to Henry.

"I certainly hope it will be the end of all this nonsense. Do you suppose the Gabrielis will be there?"

"I hope not. I do not wish anyone else to witness my humiliation."

"No, of course not," he said half-heartedly.

The courtroom was overflowing with men dressed in black, their heads topped with white wigs. Some of the wigs were placed off-center while others appeared to overtake the head on which they were perched. The judge was seated high on a dais and looking extremely bored. Bevie's legs shook as Mr. Forsythe helped her to the front of the room. She sat down and tried to think of something pleasant in order to keep from weeping.

She vaguely heard the opening statements, but her mind had long since refused to comprehend the proceedings. Only when Mr. Forsythe surprised the court with new evidence and the crowd seemed to be involved, did she snap back into the present.

"The evidence shows that another party with somewhat small footprints was present on the day of the murder," she heard Mr. Forsythe say. "We have reason to believe it was none other than Mrs. Busslingthorpe. I ask Mr. Styles to step forward and present the evidence in the form of one of the aforementioned woman's slippers that matches the form of the footprint."

At that point, those present began to chatter loudly and some made loud remarks about the inefficiency of the local detectives.

"And," Mr. Forsythe held up his hand for silence and continued, "it is entirely possible that the person who came suddenly upon the deceased, fired the Victoria pistol from the terrace causing the bullet to enter Lord Burnside from the back, which is altogether in agreement with the coroner's report. The suspect then retreated by way of the terrace and along the flower bed as is seen by the footprints coming and going along the wall. The bullet hole in the door, my lords, was the most obvious clue to the murder which was entirely overlooked by the – er – reprehensibly irresponsible prosecution."

The crowd exhibited a noise similar to the roar of a train speeding past.

Bevie observed many of the men standing, pointing their fingers, or shaking their fists at the prosecution team. She was vaguely aware that someone was calling for a postponement until further evidence could be examined. At the same time, there was an even greater commotion at the rear of the room. Everyone turned to stare at a young man who was running toward the bench at the front.

"Good heavens, it's William," Bevie said to Mr. Forsythe.

Mr. Forsythe made a dash forward in an attempt to stop William's unheard-of intrusion, but was unable to reach him before he stood in front of the judge.

"I beg your pardon, my lords, but I must make a confession. It was the bullet from my gun that went through the glass door and killed my friend, Lord Burnside. It was a hunting accident. I was so distraught that I hid my gun in the garden shed at Burnside Court. I am the one who should be on trial here – surely not this innocent lady."

Bevie could not keep quiet. "William, no!" she shouted.

Bedlam broke out in the courtroom and Lord Hampden stepped up and asked permission to speak. When the people finally quieted, he began.

"My lords, it has long since been determined by the investigators that neither of the bullets found in the body of the deceased were, nor could they have been, fired from this young man's rare and unusual hunting gun."

William was stunned. "But – they said – I thought. . ."

The judge pounded his gavel. "Sit down, young man! It is very noble of you to attempt to save your – er – well, whoever she is to you. It is highly irregular to do so in such a manner as you have done. However, under these unseemly circumstances, we shall overlook your behavior. Now I must insist on a postponement of this debacle. I shall also wish to know the reason for the incompetence of the local magistrate."

Mr. Forsythe shared a knowing smile with Henry and Mr. Hydemark, all of them certain that Constable Green was soon to receive his just dues.

It was a quiet ride home for Bevie. Everyone seemed to be taken up with their own thoughts. She thought of poor William who had been struggling under the guilty impression that he had killed her father. "No wonder he wanted to marry me," she said aloud.

"Who wants to marry you?" Max demanded to know.

"Oh – William has been pestering me to marry him. I suppose he thought to make it up to me since he thought he had killed my father."

"That young upstart! He had no right to offer for you without first seeking my approval. I shall have a stern word with him."

"Don't take such offense, sir. He was most assuredly simply obeying the dictates of his hysterical mother. He is a goose, you see."

"Is he, now? I did not know," Max said laughing at the distraught young woman. "I want you to give it up, Bevie."

"Give up what, sir?"

"Actually, I order you to give up two things. First, you must give up worrying about this situation. Secondly, you must give up calling me Lord Hampden and sir. I am Max to you."

Bevie sighed and settled down into the seat. "Yes, Max. Just tell me what will next transpire regarding my trial."

"Nothing if I have anything to say to it."

CHAPTER THIRTEEN

"Not since I was sunk in the pit of despair myself have I seen anyone so badly in need of cheering, Bevie," Pet said as she pulled Bevie out of the chaise lounge. "Exercise is always good for the mind. Come outside and walk to the pond with us. Henry is insistent on our getting some fresh air."

"Go ahead with Henry, Pet. I refuse to be a third party."

"To be perfectly honest, Bev, I believe we need a chaperone. There would be no one to protect him if I should happen to get a closer look at his handsome face. There, you see! You are smiling already – even the thought of fresh air has helped. By the way, William has called, but Max has sent him away. He told him you were resting."

"Max is getting far too protective. He is beginning to act like my father."

"Listen to yourself, Bev. It is his duty to protect you. Do you know what I think?"

"I am terribly afraid to ask."

"I believe he is falling for you."

"Nonsense. He was my father's friend."

"Very well, say what you please, but you must admit I have always had an astute sense about these things. Remember when Yolanda wanted to sink her hooks into Rodger and I told you that he was already head-over-heels for Jasmine? Well, you see I was right and no one else seemed to realize it until he persuaded Jasmine to elope with him."

"I suppose, but perhaps it was coincidence."

"I hear Henry coming down the hallway. Please come with us, Bev."

"Oh alright, if you insist. Allow me to get my wrap."

Bevie went in search of her shawl and ran directly into Max. "I have been searching for you, Bevie. I want to have a word with you about William."

"Pet told me you sent him away. It wasn't necessary for you to do so. I have been dealing with William since I was five years old. I shan't allow him to talk me into doing anything foolish."

"I should hope not because I have plans for you when all of this is behind us."

"What kind of plans?"

"I wish to give you a season. You should have had one two years ago."

"Father begged me to allow his friend, Lady Renshaw, to present me to society, but I refused. I have never wanted to attend the routs, balls, and so forth. It is all a great nuisance to me."

"What is it that you would like to do? You cannot simply shrink from life in this place."

"I don't know, Max. I suppose I want to mourn the loss of my father in peace and without a trial hanging over me."

"Yes, of course. I understand and respect your feelings."

Henry called to her. "Are you coming, Bevie? Pet won't set foot out of the house without you. She is afraid of me, I think."

Bevie laughed. "We are going for a walk, Max. Come with us, please. I don't want to be the odd person."

"Very well, but I don't think you are at all odd."

"So very kind of you to say so. What do you really think of me?" she asked as they picked up the pace and caught up with Pet and Henry.

"That you are an outspoken little chit. Do you believe it is proper to ask me such a thing?"

"You are my protector and supposedly standing in for my father. If you are very much regretting your decision to take on my situation, I wish to relieve you of that burden. I appreciate all you have done, and I confess that I could not get through the trial without your help, but when that is behind us, I want you to feel free to go back to. . . wherever it is you desire to go."

Max stopped in his tracks. "Let me say that it seems as if you are trying to get rid of me. I am devastated. I was sadly operating under the false assumption that we were a team."

Bevie turned back toward him and searched his face. The last thing she wanted was to hurt him after all he had done for her. Then she discovered a twinkle in his eye and a smile escaping from the corners of his mouth. "You are bamming me, Max. Admit it – you do like me a little."

"Yes, brat, I do like you a little and I'm not going anywhere."

A brisk wind began to blow. "Let's return to the house, Bevie. The last thing you need at this juncture is to take a chill."

"Where are Pet and Henry? We should not leave them out here alone."

"Oh, I feel certain they will be perfectly alright."

"Perhaps you are correct, but Pet will not be happy with me."

They had just turned back toward the house when they heard a scream.

"That's Pet. Oh, Max, what have I done? I've left her alone with that monster." She began to run in the direction of the scream, but Max caught her arm and held her back.

"Wait, Bevie. Here they come."

Pet was jumping up and down along the path and dragging Henry along with her.

Bevie ran toward them. "What is it, Pet? Has something terrible happened?"

"Something wonderful has happened, Bev. Henry has proposed!"

"You gave us a fright with your screaming." Bevie put her arms around her friend and hugged her. "I am so happy for both of you. I suppose that negates your resolve to distance yourself from all men," she said, laughing.

Max was shaking Henry's hand. "Why, you sly fox. All this time we imagined you had your nose buried in those books in the library."

Henry held onto Pet's hand tightly as they walked to the house, seemingly afraid to let his butterfly escape.

The foursome ambled toward the house. Bevie noticed some spring blooms and suddenly had a glimmer of hope that her nightmare would eventually end. She stumbled and Max caught her before she fell.

At the same moment, their attention was drawn to the sound of someone trampling through the woods. They searched through the trees trying to identify the intruder. Bevie caught a glimpse of the same figure she had seen fleeing through the wooded area near where she and William sat on the stone wall.

"There he is again. It is the same man I saw running from me several days ago. Do you think he is a poacher?"

"I am sure that is exactly what he is," Max tried to assure her, although he believed the reason for the man's presence was probably a great deal more sinister than that of a poacher. He made a mental note to hire more guards.

As soon as they reached the house, Max went in search of his hired men and then asked Mrs. Metterson to find Cecil. He had a notion that the man in the woods might have been Cecil. The man wore a coat with a cape which had blown or been placed over his head and, thus, defied recognition.

"You asked to see me?" Cecil questioned Max as he entered the drawing room.

"I was wondering if you have recently been out walking on the estate."

"No, why do you ask?"

"It seems we may have a poacher prowling about. I thought you may have seen him."

Now that Cecil stood before him, Max mentally placed him beside the man he had seen in the woods and realized Cecil was much smaller, even supposing the intruder had several layers of clothing covering him.

"I haven't been out since we returned. When is the will to be read?"

"Assuming the codicil is located, it is my understanding that things will be settled immediately after the trial is over. Much depends on the outcome, you see."

"No, I do not see. How does the outcome of the trial affect the reading of the will?"

"I have been led to believe that Bevie is somehow mentioned in the will, if only that she should receive a settlement of some sort. In the event that she is found guilty, it would alter the distribution."

"By that do you mean to say that I would inherit the estate?"

"Perhaps, but I absolutely have not had the privilege of seeing the will. Do you suppose you are to inherit all of it?"

"Of course I do. I am the next in line for the title. What man in his right mind would want his successor to bear his title and no lands?"

"Hmmm, a very good question, Cecil."

Max excused himself and went to hire more guards. He had deliberately baited Cecil to see if he would take some action to try to prove Bevie's guilt. As he passed the library, he noticed Pet and Henry whispering the corner.

"Hello, you two love-birds," he said, announcing his presence.

"Come in, Lord Hampden, we were just discussing our future. Pet would not consider a wedding without her best friend in attendance. It seems we shall have to wait until she is out of her blacks."

"Too kind, I'm sure. I do have a request to make of you. I know you do not wish to be separated for a moment, but I believe we are at a critical point as far as Bevie's safety is concerned. I am very uneasy about the person we saw creeping about in the woods. Here is what I am asking." Max outlined his plan.

Cecil climbed the stairs two at a time and barged into his mother's room.

"What do you want, Cecil. I am feeling out of sorts."

"You are always out of sorts, Mother. Take a holiday from the vapors until we discuss what is to be done."

"Do not be disrespectful to your mother, Cecil."

Cecil ignored her and began his diatribe. "Nothing you have suggested has had the slightest bearing on the outcome we seek. Now I shall say what is to be done. I have information that leads me to believe that the codicil has not been found. We shall write one and pretend to discover it under the nose of that stilted marquess. My friend from Oxford has agreed to draw it up. In the meantime, you shall go into the library and take every single piece of paper you can find with Burnside's signature on it. Then you shall practice writing in his exact hand."

"I am not very well and I do not write as splendidly as some of the gentry."

"Stop whining, Mother, or pack your bags and go home. It is my future we are discussing."

"What about my future, dear boy?" she whimpered.

"You will be . . . no doubt you will be alright provided you do your part in this. I am leaving immediately. Do not fail me, Mother."

With that, Cecil stormed out of the house and went to the stables to saddle his horse. Henry Pick watched with interest as one of the hired men quickly mounted his horse and followed Cecil at a distance.

Mrs. Jackson sat on the window seat in the hallway just outside Araminta Busslingthorpe's room, holding a lavender-scented handkerchief, ready to dab her head and pretend a faint if the woman should suddenly come out of her chamber. Pet instructed one of the footmen as to where to set up the extra bed in Bevie's room. It would be hers until the danger had passed. She would not let Bevie out of her sight.

Mrs. Metterson had been told on more than one occasion that she had eyes in the back of her head. Hardly a person stepped foot on the estate but what she knew it. She chided herself over the fact that she had not been able to determine the identity of the caped man in the woods, nor had she once seen him.

Mrs. Metterson and Mr. Hydemark stood on the terrace surveying the area. "I must be losing my touch, Hayden, she admitted. It is seldom that something of this nature slips by me unnoticed. However, I shall keep a sharp eye out for any intruders."

"Rest easy, Mina. We have always worked well together and I feel certain we shall uncover this mystery before the week is over. I am of the opinion that you are the most astute detective in the city. Pity that you were born a woman or we would have very few unsolved crimes – not that you do not make a very attractive woman," he quickly added.

"You are too generous by far, Hayden, but I do thank you for the compliment."

"Has the maid returned after her second absence or sent for her pay?"

"I do not believe so. She seemed distraught over the fact that she had somehow failed Lady Beverley. Perhaps she will return after the trial."

"I sincerely hope Mrs. Jackson will not take her back on staff."

"She is rather incompetent as a lady's maid, but she did seem devoted to Lady Beverley."

"Perhaps, but not to my satisfaction."

Max paced the floor while Bevie and Pet sat side-by-side on the settee in the library.

"I cannot like this business of Pet having to be attached to my hip, sir. She has her own life to live, particularly now that she and Henry are engaged to be married."

"Hush, darling," Pet whispered. "I will not have you think that there could be anyone more concerned for your safety. I have no doubt you would do the same for me."

Max paced again. "I need to think. I have missed some important clue, but my mind will not obey me and bring it to the forefront. When was the last time you saw this fellow, Hughes, Bevie?"

"To tell the truth, I hardly ever saw him. He seemed to slither in and out of the library during the day and disappear each night. Father allowed him full swing of the estate, I believe. Now I can see that it was a mistake to do so, but hindsight . . . we all know about it."

"Yes, of course. Now, Bevie, are you absolutely certain you had never before laid eyes on Busslingthorpe or his mother?"

"Of that I am certain, Max. Who could miss that flaming-red hair?"

"Perhaps he wore a hat."

"I would have remembered him."

"Quite so," Max remarked as he stroked his chin.

Mr. Hydemark tapped on the library door and interrupted his thoughts. "I am going to the chapel to pray and wondered if anyone wished to go along."

Bevie jumped up. "Yes, I would like it above all things, Mr. Hydemark."

Max frowned. "I fear we cannot take the chance of your being out of the house where someone might per chance be able to harm you, Bevie."

"What if God's eyes are on me. Wouldn't that be far better?"

"You put me to shame and have certainly backed me into a corner. Very well, then let us all go together. Perhaps a little prayer asking the Lord to allow my brain to work in a more efficient fashion would be just the thing."

The chapel was in walking distance of the house along the carriage roadway. Everyone flanked Bevie so that no marksman would be able to aim at her. One of Max's men stepped out of his pre-determined post along the way and greeted them.

Pet smiled at the way Max held onto Bevie as though she were a china doll. Mr. Hydemark led the way to the front of the chapel where he immediately kneeled down.

"Please lead us all in a prayer, if you wouldn't mind, Mr. Hydemark. After that we shall struggle to put our own thoughts into words," Bevie requested. They all kneeled.

On the way back, Max walked with his arm around Bevie. She decided she liked the idea of having a handsome protector. Mr. Hydemark and Pet walked behind them and smiled at each other, their thoughts all spoken in the smiles.

They heard the sound of a horse approaching at a gallop and once again gathered around Bevie to protect her. When the horseman came within sight, Bevie said, "Relax, it is only William."

He reined in his horse in front of them. "What is this? You look as though you think I am ready to kidnap Bevie. I assure you I am not foolish enough to try that again."

"We only wanted to be sure who was coming at us at such a furious clip. What is your hurry, William?"

"I am coming to speak to you privately, Lord Hampden."

"Follow us back to the house, William. I shall meet you in the library," Max offered.

"Thank you, sir."

"Wait, William. I wish to say that I think you did a very brave thing in the courtroom," Bevie mentioned. "It was very noble of you to try to save me, but why did you not tell me what was troubling you."

"Surely you don't have to ask, Bev. I thought I had accidentally killed your father. I was beside myself."

"I am sorry you had to suffer under that misconception."

Pet and Bevie escaped to their bed chamber while William waited nervously for Max to enter the library. There was no doubt in anyone's mind about the nature of his mission. Bevie hoped Max would handle the matter gently without hurting William's feelings.

Max fully intended to push the deed off on his ward since she assured him she had been handling William since she was five years old. "After all, I am not a father. I do not have any experience in these things," Max said aloud to himself as he reluctantly approached the library. He hesitated, took a deep breath, and entered.

"Have a seat, William. What can I do for you?"

"Well, sir, you are surely aware of the fact that I have known Bevie since we were children. I have a very high regard for her and I believe I would make a very reliable husband. I only need your permission to court her, sir."

"Yes, of course. Am I to understand that you have presented your suit to Bevie before?"

William hesitated before he answered. "I suppose you understand that I was trying to get both of us out of harm's way, so to speak. I believed I had killed her father and that she was taking the – that is, being charged with the crime. I thought if we both disappeared, it would solve both problems. But now I wish to marry her so that we might have a life together, you see."

"What kind of a life would you have together if she is convicted of murder? Do you believe she did it, William?"

The shocked look on William's face almost made Max laugh.

"How can you even suggest it, Lord Hampden? She loved her father more than. . . I suppose, more than anyone."

"Who do you suppose is the murderer?"

"Most likely Busslingthorpe. He has the most to gain."

"Yes, quite. What would you gain by marrying her, William?"

It was the question he dreaded. He tried to force his gaze to remain calm and not divert his eyes, but he could not contain the color that insisted upon rising from his neck to his face. He hoped he would be convincing when he said, "Why, a wife, sir. That is the idea, is it not?"

"May I ask if you might be willing to have me meet with your banker to ascertain your ability to take care of my ward?"

William stood up and cleared his throat. "It is true that I am not – shall I say – flush at the moment, sir, but in time I will inherit from my uncle as I am his heir."

"Allow me to lay the matter on the table, William. You may have my permission to court Bevie after the trial has concluded, assuming she is found to be innocent. However, she must be the one to decide whether or not she is agreeable to the idea."

"That is most kind of you, sir. May I ask her now?"

"Let us arrange for you to meet her tomorrow afternoon at three. She is being guarded every minute and I cannot allow you to see her alone. Is that understood?"

"Yes, sir. Thank you, sir."

William took his leave wondering exactly how much money Bevie would receive in the settlement. He did not suffer the slightest tinge of guilt over being a fortune-hunter since most of the gentlemen of the *ton* married for the very same reason.

CHAPTER FOURTEEN

Bevie's new trial date was set for two days hence. For that reason, she sent a note to say that she would be unable to receive William the following afternoon. "At least I can be spared that unpleasantness for the moment," she told Pet.

"You would not consider his offer, would you, Bev?"

"Of course not, you ninny. I thought I might at one time simply because I was afraid of who and what Max might be. Now that I know him, I realize he has my best interest in mind."

"I am sure he has much more than that in mind, Bev. Are you blind?"

"I am very practical. He is here as a favor to my father and he feels obligated to do everything he can to see that I land on my feet after this extraordinary event. I am very thankful for that."

"As am I, darling, but we must concentrate on discovering who would dare to harm your father. Think very hard, Bev. He had an enemy and we must expose the villain."

"I am sorry that I wasn't more attentive to things that were unfolding in the household. I suppose there was no way I could have known his friends on the outside. It must have been one of them. As far as I know, he wasn't a gambler, so it could not have been that sort of a thing. Suppose he was a spy of some kind, Pet. I wouldn't have known about that either."

"We must not reach beyond what is reasonable. I have a feeling that Mr. Hydemark is onto something. He really is an exceptional man. I wonder why he has never married."

"He is too busy helping everyone else and taking care of – I suppose you could say – God's things."

"Yes, that is exactly the case."

Their conversation ended when someone tapped on the door of their bedchamber. Pet cautiously opened it to find one of the new guards ready to escort Bevie to the library where Lord Struthers was meeting with Max and wished to speak with her.

"It seems utterly ridiculous to have an escort from my bedchamber to the library," she told the guard.

"Lord Hampden's orders, miss. The place is large enough to have intruders."

"I suppose you are correct."

"I will leave you here, miss," he said as he opened the library door for her.'

She curtsied to Lord Struthers.

"Let us sit and confer on the matter at hand, Lady Beverley. I wish for you to relax and let your mind wander to the past when you may have had contact with some important peer of the realm. It seems that someone in the House of Lords has unduly influenced others in the matter of your guilt."

Bevie was alarmed. "It sounds very ominous and certainly must be for you to be concerned about it, Lord Struthers."

"Yes, it would seem that your future may rest on your memory, my dear."

They all remained quiet. Bevie suddenly stood up. "There was a time when Lord Abernathy attempted to arrange a marriage between his odious son, Herbert de Camp, and me. My father was outraged and refused, but Lord Abernathy persisted and threatened to ruin us financially if he did not comply. My father mentioned to me that he believed Abernathy had lost his estate in a card game."

"My dear girl, why did you not reveal this before?"

"I hadn't thought about it since it happened. I was not dreadfully upset because my father sheltered me from nearly everything that was unpleasant."

"Quite appropriately so. What was the outcome of the meeting? Did your father say?"

"No, but I listened from the hallway while my father laughed at him and told him to get out or he would throw him out."

"Since there has been no new evidence, it is imperative that we do some damage control, Max. I believe you must contact everyone you know in the House of Lords and explain the situation while I do the same. It will have to be done before the onset of the trial. I fear we may have let this matter go unattended for too long."

Bevie's frightened eyes looked into Max's concerned ones. There was no help for her there. "What can I do?"

"Nothing, my dear," said Lord Struthers. "We shall handle the situation as best we are able. Come, Max, we must be about our business."

Max called for the guard to escort Bevie back to her room. She insisted on finding Mr. Hydemark and asking him to pray with her.

Bevie lay in her bed praying all through the night. She had no hope but the mercy of God. Sleep forsook her and she was up and dressed before the fires were lit. She quietly stepped over the guard who had fallen asleep outside her door. The breakfast room was empty and devoid of the smell of morning coffee. She considered going for an early morning ride, but decided against it.

She heard footsteps in the hallway. Max entered the breakfast room. "I've hurried them along with breakfast. You must try to eat."

"I have no appetite. Will you go for a ride with me? I wish to ride Serenity one last time before. . ."

"We must remain positive, Bevie. I fear it is too dangerous for us to be out in the open."

"Will you promise to take care of Serenity if I have to. . ."

"Yes, of course, but I am certain you will be around to ride her each and every day that suits you."

"I only wish I could believe it."

The time for the trial arrived quickly. Bevie was dazed as she sat and listened to various people accuse her of murder. She wondered why God had not brought about justice. She thought of something Mr. Hydemark had pressed her to remember. They were words of comfort that Jesus Christ had spoken to his disciples.

The prosecution began arguing that no new evidence had been uncovered and, therefore, the jury must decide the case based on what was known, namely that one of the weapons used in the murder was found in Lady Beverley's room and that she was discovered at the murder scene.

"What more in the way of evidence would any jury need?" demanded the prosecutor. "The offense is one that requires a life for a life," he added.

Bevie's heart plummeted to her feet when she heard his words. That could only mean she would be hung. She refused to imagine it.

The jury delivered a guilty verdict. The sentence was death. Bevie wept. Tears streamed down the faces of Max, Pet, and everyone who knew of her innocence. Court was adjourned and Lord Struthers immediately demanded a private meeting with the judge.

Bevie was held by guards and told to remain where she sat. Everyone else was escorted from the room, but Max refused to leave her side. A half hour passed which seemed like an eternity to Bevie. Max told her that the sentence would be vigorously disputed by Lord Struthers.

Presently, the judge and Lord Struthers returned to the courtroom and announced that the death sentence had been reduced to deportment based on the fact that no motive for the murder had been found. In addition to that, the actual cause of death had not been determined. It was uncertain whether poisoning or one of the bullets had ended the man's life.

Bevie was too numb to regard the implications of the change in her sentencing. She was simply led from the courtroom to the outside. She was surprised when she was helped up into Lord Struthers' carriage and Max sat beside her.

"You have been released into the custody of Lord Struthers until arrangements can be made for you to travel to the destination yet to be named by the court," Max informed her.

"It is all the same to me, Max. It might have been better if they had lopped off my head and finished it."

"Stop that talk and listen to me. I will not leave you alone. Wherever they send you I will follow. Is that clear?"

"Don't be silly, Max. You are not being deported. They shall place me in the hold of one of those ships which transports depraved people to the ends of the earth and I shall no doubt perish before I arrive at some distant place where no one wishes to live. Do not think I am so stupid and sheltered that I do not know of these things."

"Hush," he said, pulling her into his arms. "I intend to fight this and search the earth until I find the murderer."

"Thank you. Why are we going to Burnside Court?"

"We will remain here for one night at which time you must pack everything you wish to take on the journey."

"How shall I know what to take if I do not know my destination?"

Max whispered in her ear. "I am thinking of asking Mr. Gabrieli if he would renew his offer to help you escape to the Continent. The thing is, Bevie, that you would have to stay there until the murderer is found and still you would be charged with defying the court's order."

"When a person is deported, does it mean they can never return to their home country?"

"Yes, I believe it does."

"Then I can see very little difference except that I could choose where I live and would no doubt have to change my identity."

"Are you willing to go along with the notion, then?"

"I am certainly considering it."

When the under-butler, who hoped to be promoted to butler, opened the door, it was apparent to the arriving group that others had come before them. Bevie did not wish to see anyone, but Pet pulled her into the drawing room where William, Nicky, Mr. Hydemark, Mrs. Jackson, Mrs. Metterson, and Henry stood talking with one another.

"We have come to support you, darling," Pet reminded her.

Mrs. Metterson closed the door as Max slipped inside. "Where is your friend, Lord Struthers?" she inquired of Max.

"He has left with his carriage and will return tomorrow to take Bevie away."

"Good, then we have the whole night to execute our plan for her escape."

Bevie looked at her friends and sighed. "I hate to run away from my problems. Father always said that we must face life head-on."

Mrs. Jackson spoke up. "If he were here, he would tell you to get away as fast as you can."

To her amazement, Bevie found herself laughing. "This looks for all the world like a kidnapping. I am so blessed to have such good friends."

"Then you will come with me?" Nicky asked.

"I believe I have no choice in the matter."

"I am your skipper. No one else will be on deck. We leave in time to catch the tide."

"I am so sorry that I will miss your wedding, Pet. Perhaps you will visit me wherever I am going. I am certain Nicky will let you know without alerting the authorities."

"I shall be unable to come to you immediately, Bevie, but I promise to join you when the rumors have ceased," Max assured her.

The conversations stopped when the under-butler entered the room and announced the arrival of Mr. Desford who carried a leather case containing the will.
"I am very sorry to hear of the most unsatisfactory conclusion reached by the court," he said to Bevie.

"Thank you."

"I have come for the reading of the will, and with many thanks to your friend, Mr. Hydemark, for locating the legal copy of the codicil."

"Do you wish to do so immediately?" Max asked.

"It will be necessary for Mr. Busslingthorpe to attend. Does he reside in the house?"

"I am certain he is hiding in some nearby crevice or rabbit hole," Max replied sarcastically.

"Then perhaps we shall convene in one hour if that is convenient."

The conspirators exchanged glances and Max nodded to Nicky who knew it was a signal for him to begin the preparations for the clandestine voyage. The ladies all went to Bevie's bedchamber with packing her belongings in mind.

They did not meet in the library. Bevie did not want to be reminded of the terrible scene whereupon she found her father lying on the floor. The sunroom was her favorite place in the house and she decided to spend her last few moments at Burnside Court thinking of the good times she had spent living in her home.

Cecil Busslingthorpe entered the room like the cat that had swallowed the proverbial canary. His nose was elevated to a new height that made Bevie wonder if he would trip over his own feet or, at least, get a crick in his neck.

Mr. Desford wasted no time declaring that Cecil would become the Sixth Earl of Burnside just as soon as the proper documentation was processed. Cecil preened and thought about the ways he would make everyone who disliked him more miserable than he had ever been made to feel.

Mr. Desford then explained that the codicil had specifically left the entire estate and all of the properties to his daughter, Beverley M. Murray, to be properly and duly managed and executed by Maximillian St. Ives, Lord Hampden, until she reached the age of five and twenty or in the case of her approved marriage.

In the event that Lady Beverley was not able to carry out the mandate, whether because of illness, death, or some unforeseen reason, Maximillian St. Ives would take full control of the estate and all of its holdings.

Generous distributions were made to all the staff, except for Mr. Hughes, who had curiously been omitted from the will. The biggest surprise came when Mr.

Desford announced that Lord Burnside had left his hunting lodge to Lord Sedley, his neighbor and very good friend.

When Cecil heard the details of the distribution of properties and moneys, he stormed out of the room and went to find his mother. His hope of inheriting the monies and the estate if Bevie were found guilty, was squelched with the declaration that Lord Hampden would have control of the entire fortune when Lady Beverley departed the country.

CHAPTER FIFTEEN

Mr. Hydemark and Max discussed the problems concerning Nicky's propensity to ignore his responsibilities whenever he sniffed entertainment in the air and the consequences that might be borne by Bevie as a result. They bantered back and forth with various ideas of how to prevent such future events until Mr. Hydemark was summoned to the drawing room where a visitor awaited his arrival.

Max followed him as far as the doorway, curious to know who was coming to visit at such a seemingly inconvenient time. He recognized the man as one of the Bow Street Runners, but deliberately said nothing about it and turned away. He went to see how Bevie and her helpers were managing the packing.

Cecil faced his mother with outrage and fury. "Who found the codicil and why wasn't the copy my friend procured delivered to Desford?"

"I am certain it was, dear boy, but he must have ignored it. Is there nothing that can be done about it?"

"How should I know? I am no barrister."

"Pity that."

"So you say, but who are you to speak of my shortcomings? Look what you have done with your life – nothing but interfere in mine."

Araminta began to cry. "I raised you, did I not?" she sobbed.

"Oh, stop your whimpering, Mother. What shall we do now?"

"Take everything you can carry away from this house. They owe it to you, dear boy."

"You take what you want, Mother. I have to decide what I am going to do. I believe I shall join up."

"And leave me alone? No such thing, dear boy. We will manage. I am going to the dining room to see what redeemable silver I can find. I shall not lift it until the small hours, but at least I'll know where the best things are kept."

Araminta calmly walked out of the room and meandered down the stairway toward the dining room. As she rounded the corner at the bottom, she ran directly into Mr. Hydemark.

"Good afternoon, Mrs. Busslingthorpe. It must be such a burden to have taken on an assumed name for so many years."

"Exactly what is the meaning of that statement? Speaking of someone who is *de trop*, Mr. Hydemark, I do not understand why you continue to snoop around when you are no longer needed or wanted."

"Yes, I see what you mean, Mrs. Bussing – excuse the error, I mean to say Miss Dingle."

The color drained from Araminta's face. "You have me confused with someone else."

"I think not. Miss Araminta Dingle, daughter of the late farmer, Deniston Dingle. What was Mr. Busslingthorpe's game? Perhaps he had another wife – or simply did not countenance being leg-shackled to you."

"You – you big. . ." She rushed at him, attempting to claw at his eyes just as the under-butler entered the hallway and pulled her away.

"This is just not done, Mrs. Busslingthorpe," the under-butler said. "Go about your business."

She turned and ran up the steps.

Mr. Hydemark hurried to the front entrance where he caught up with Mr. Desford in time to save him another trip to Burnside Court. Having acted as a solicitor at one time, Mr. Hydemark was fully aware that an illegitimate son, regardless of his relationship to his predecessor, could not inherit the title of Earl of Burnside. He had suspected and finally had proof that Araminta had never married Mr. Busslingthorpe. In fact, he had also learned that there were rumors to the effect that she had pushed the fellow off a cliff to his untimely death.

Mr. Desford dismounted and patted Mr. Hydemark on the back. "You are one of the best, Hydemark. Wish you'd come and work for me. I knew that woman was beyond all that is decent. In fact, as I told you, I was certain from the outset that she had something to do with the false codicil that was delivered to me last night. I only hope the magistrate sends someone to arrest those imposters before they disappear."

"I did not have a chance to ask you how you discovered the Busslingthorpes' connection to the false papers."

"It seems the young solicitor who Busslingthorpe hired to make the document began to have an attack of conscience.   More to the point, I believe he was frightened that he would ruin his career if his treachery were to be discovered."

Their conversation was interrupted by the arrival of a police wagon and two officers of the law. They strode past, nodding to the two men as they approached the footman at the door. Mr. Hydemark and Mr. Desford leaned up against a hitching-post and watched to see what would unfold.

Ten minutes later, the officers appeared with Cecil and Araminta in tow. Naturally, Araminta was screaming obscenities at the officers. The two were pushed into the back of the wagon and driven off to await their uncertain future.

"Who will inherit the title now?" Hydemark inquired.

"I have done some investigation concerning the matter. The young man is six years old and comes along the line of Burnside's grandfather. His family seems to be well-heeled and the lack of inherited money will not be detrimental to him in any way."

"I find that reassuring."

"Well, that's that, is it not, Hydemark?"

"Not quite. We still have an innocent who has been falsely charged with murder."

"Indeed. I feel certain something will make it come right-about."

"Oh, one other thing, Desford. Will our Bevie forfeit all of the inherited property and monies since she was convicted of murder?"

"I intend to delay the distribution as long as possible. Perhaps the real villain will turn up soon."

"I do pray you are correct. Good-day, Desford, and give my regards to your lovely wife."

Pet was the one to break the news of Cecil and Araminta's arrest.

"I am gratified to know that the law got one thing right," Bevie said bitterly.

"Don't fret, my dear friend. Nicky will take good care of you until my wonderful Henry discovers the truth."

"Will you come to visit me, Pet?"

"Of course, darling. Have no fear on that account, only that we must wait until we are certain it will not put you in jeopardy."

Bevie did not care what she took with her, nor did she care to think about leaving Burnside Court forever. She was beginning to have second thoughts about running away.

"Where do you suppose the court would send me, Mrs. Metterson?" Bevie vaguely inquired as she stared out the window.

"I don't know, dear. They have been turning away from sending people to the colonies due to the unrest over there. Perhaps they would send you to Australia or the islands."

"I think I could get used to the islands."

"But you would be put in a position of indentured servant, Bevie. Do you not see how horrible it would be?"

"Yes, I had forgotten that."

After that brutal reminder, Bevie was committed to leaving England and going wherever Nicky decided would be a safe hiding place.

"Why don't you marry Mr. Hydemark, Mrs. Metterson?"

"My dear girl, what in the world prompted that question?"

"You seem to suit."

"Mr. Hydemark is a dear friend and we have worked together for some time – nothing more than that, Bevie."

"Then there must be someone else. You are too attractive to avoid the gentlemen's notice."

"I have had my moments. To be truthful, the one man I wished to marry chose someone else."

"Aaahh, unrequited love, is it?" Pet injected. I know something of that state of unhappiness. Perhaps it is time for you to move on. Nicky has a very handsome friend who is a little older, but. . ."

"Stop, my dears. I must admit that I was once married and do not wish to marry again now or ever. I am perfectly happy as I am."

Bevie still stared out the window trying to memorize the lay of the estate as if to burn it into her memory.

"Look! Come here all of you! That is the man I saw in the woods earlier." Bevie alerted the group of ladies as she pointed to a dark figure moving along the line of trees. The man, who was wearing a black cape, hurried through the wooded area and soon disappeared from sight.

"I must tell Lord Hampden that he has a poacher," announced Mrs. Jackson. "That will never do."

"Poachers do not wear such clothing, do they?" asked Pet.

Mrs. Metterson gasped, "He looked satanic to me."

Moments later, Max and Mrs. Jackson appeared below Bevie's window. Max called up to her. "Which way did he go?"

Bevie opened the window and pointed in the direction she had last seen the man. "He is the same person I saw earlier," she called to Max.

Several minutes later, three of Max's hired men appeared on horseback. He spoke instructions and they each went through the woods in a different direction. They returned later to say they had not found the intruder.

The packing was complete and the ladies left Bevie alone. Her stomach began to tighten as the realization of what she was doing pressed in on her. She had a strong desire to see her horse, Serenity, once more before she left.

She opened her door and spoke to the guard outside, asking him to accompany her to the stables. He saw no reason to deny her wish and they hurried along the short path to the meadow where Serenity nibbled on the new shoots of spring grass. Bevie leaned on the fence and called to her. The horse nuzzled her snout into Bevie's neck. Bevie began to weep.

One of the stable hands called to the guard to investigate a commotion he heard taking place above the stable. The guard was torn between staying by his charge or protecting her from anything that might be happening in the stable that could potentially threaten her safety. He instructed her to remain where she stood while he went to check on the situation.

It happened so quickly that Bevie did not have time to be frightened. A sack was thrown over her head and she was hoisted onto a horse and spirited away from the area. Her kidnapper was rough and she wondered if she would survive the ordeal. Before long, she was lowered to the ground and pulled along by two people who each held one of her arms. She tried desperately to see through the thick material as they shoved her into a place she assumed was a building. A man with a gravelly voice spoke of leaving and she heard bolts being thrown. Her other captor guided her to a seat and pulled the sack from her head.

"Herbert de Camp, you odious man! What do you want with me?"

Herbert uttered an evil laugh. "I thought I wanted to marry you, but I have since reconsidered. Now, I only want your money and you as a temporary playmate without the nightmare of having to be leg-shackled to a simpering female."

"Really, Herbert, I knew when your father tried to force our marriage that you had little or no gumption, but I never dreamed it was full-blown cowardice."

"Shut up!" he said, knocking her to the floor.

Bevie began to realize that he was desperate and probably on the verge of insanity. She decided to change her strategy since he evidently had not heard of her impending deportation. "Well, I have thought about your offer, Herbert. Now that my father is gone, perhaps you would reconsider our marriage."

He looked at her with shock. "Why would I want to marry you?"

"For my money, of course."

"Yes, well, there is that. How much is there. Did Busslingthorpe get most of it?"

"I actually cannot say since the settlement has not occurred. Of course, if I am missing, there could be a change that could possibly make Cecil Busslingthorpe the recipient of the entire estate. I assure you he would not be willing to share it with you."

"I suppose that could be true."

The thought suddenly struck Bevie that he could have been her father's murderer. She endeavored to learn the truth. If he admitted to it, she felt that she might do likewise to him. She approached the subject. "It would have been better if you had reasoned with my father. There was no need to kill him."

"Don't be daft. I did not kill him, although the thought did cross my mind."

"Your father, then?"

"As to that, I cannot say. I have broken faith with the man. He refused to give me any of his precious blunt."

"I see. How very awful for you. Perhaps there is another way."

"What?"

"Suppose I agreed to set you up in business."

"What do you take me for? My man has already delivered the ransom note. I don't need your charity."

"Then leave me alone, Herbert."

"Oh no, my dear. You will make a tasty morsel."

Max was thunderstruck when the guard told him what had happened. He ran for the stables while shouting orders to his men. When he reached the place where the guard told him Bevie had been standing, he got down and attempted to find the footprints of the kidnapper. Failing that, he had another idea. He took Serenity out of the meadow and quickly put a harness on her. He stroked her neck and whispered in her ear. "Find Bevie, girl. I know you can do it." He proceeded to allow the horse to lead him into the woods.

Three of his men were on their horses surrounding him and thought he was a few cards short of a deck – expecting a horse to find Bevie. Nevertheless, they followed as the horse wandered through the trees, stopping to munch a few choice pieces of grass every so often. Presently, they came to a clearing which was surrounded by several cottages.

"She is being held in one of these," Max announced.

The men exchanged pitiful glances and rolled their eyes.

"Dismount, draw your weapons, and follow me," he commanded in a near-whisper.

Serenity edged toward one of the cottages and stopped. Max let her go and motioned for the men to follow him. He crouched down under a dirty window and listened for the sound of Bevie's voice.

He heard a man shouting, "I wouldn't do anything foolish if I were you."

Bevie picked up the chair and threw it at Herbert.

When Max heard the crash, he motioned for the men to follow him to the door which they broke down with a collective effort. Max immediately observed that Bevie had not been harmed, but saw her captor pointing a gun at her.

"Hold hard boys!" Max ordered.

Herbert was momentarily confused, but quickly took hold of Bevie and held her in front of him as a hostage. "Stay back or I'll kill her," he shouted.

Max's men were decorated ex-military compatriots and nearly laughed at the amateur kidnapper. Two of them created a diversion while the other one struck Herbert in the head with the butt of a gun. Herbert swayed and fell into a heap.

"Tie him up and leave him here. I'll send the law after him," Max ordered.

Bevie was shaking when Max lifted her onto the bare back of her heroine, Serenity. Bevie leaned forward, kissed her, and sweet-talked her all the way back to Burnside Court. She promised her oats, an apple, and many sugar cubes.

She was still shaking when Max lifted her down. Just then the full impact of what had taken place hit her and she began to cry.

Max held her tightly. "I so wish I could come with you tonight, Bevie. I hate to leave you with that Gabrieli fellow."

"If only you could come, Max. I feel so safe with you."

"I promise I will come to you just as soon as I have put things in order here and in Yorkshire. Let us go inside now and try to pretend that we expect you to leave with Lord Struthers in the morning. I fear he will suspect that we have collaborated against him with this sad venture."

"Will he mind terribly, Max? I know he is a good friend of yours and he has done everything possible to help me."

"He will forgive me – eventually."

CHAPTER SIXTEEN

Bevie sat in front of the smoldering fire in her private sitting room thinking about her pending journey. Someone tapped lightly on her door and her guard announced the footman.

"I'm here to collect your boxes, My Lady."

Bevie took him into her bedchamber and pointed to the few things she planned to take with her, pushing aside most of the bags the ladies had packed.

"Is that all, miss?"

"Yes, Jenkins, that will be all."

"Thank you, miss," he said, bowing before he took his leave. "We all knowed you didn't do it."

"Yes, thank you, Jenkins."

Before the door closed, Mr. Hydemark stepped inside. "A word with you, please, Lady Beverley."

"Do not bother to say it, Mr. Hydemark. I have been thinking that I am going in the wrong direction and that I am a great disappointment to God."

Mr. Hydemark nodded to the guard and closed the door. "May we sit?" he asked.

"Please, and tell me how I will explain my change of plans to Max and the others. I must admit that I am very fearful of allowing the court to dictate my future."

"The Scripture clearly tells us to obey the law. I know they are entirely wrong in their verdict, Bevie, but you must remember that God is in charge of your life. He undoubtedly has some reason for allowing this to happen."

"But what?"

"I confess I do not understand it."

"By this time, my bags will be on the way to Nicky's boat – or ship - or whatever it is."

"It is hardly of consequence since the authorities would not allow you to take those things with you when you are escorted onto the ship that will take you to your destination. I, however, have a plan. I shall engage in some footwork and endeavor to learn which ship will be yours. I intend to book passage and come along."

"I would never want to put you to that trouble and expense, Mr. Hydemark, but I do thank you for helping me. Now, if you will go and explain my situation to the others, I will be even more indebted to you."

Mr. Hydemark bowed and left Bevie in a daze. Evening was approaching and dinner would soon be served. Bevie asked the guard to have a tray sent to her room. She could not face the others with her decision to bend to the court's dictates.

Max threw a book at the fireplace. "What has possessed her to decide such a thing? She will be ruined – that is, if she ever arrives at her destination alive. Half of the prisoners will die en route."

Mr. Hydemark was glad Pet was not present to hear the news. She had taken leave for a short time to tend to some of her own affairs.

Mrs. Jackson would not accept Bevie's decision. "I must speak with her and make her see what folly it is."

"Not just now, Mrs. Jackson. I believe I should have a word with her," said Max. "I cannot allow her to do this."

"I agree," offered Henry.

"I am not sure," said Mrs. Metterson. "I must admit that Mr. Hydemark tends to be in tune with whatever God has in mind. Perhaps he and Bevie have the right of it."

"Thank you for telling us, Hydemark. Now if you will all excuse me, I need to think." Max dismissed them. "Wait, Henry, remain here with me, if you will."

After the others had left, Max sat down, leaned over and put his head in his hands. "I cannot allow her to do this, Henry. I am going to need your help. We will have to kidnap her and put her on Nicky's boat."

"I am in total agreement. When shall we do it?"

"The original plan was for her to leave at three on the clock. Let us surprise her at two."

Mr. Hydemark made a call at Lord Struthers' residence where he learned the name of the prisoner's ship. Naturally, Lord Struthers was not aware of the many plans, twists, and turns with regard to Bevie's situation. He fully expected Bevie to comply with the court's decision. He was alarmed at her recent kidnapping by Herbert de Camp and admitted that he thought it might have been best if Herbert had managed to keep her captive until after the ship left harbor.

"It's not the worst ship I've seen, but I am still concerned about the treatment she will receive. She will be with the ilk of society, you see," Lord Struthers explained.

"Is there a possibility you could arrange for me to be – oh, for instance – a chaplain on board the ship?"

"Are you sure you want to do this, Hydemark? It could take years off your life."

"My life is in God's hands and my days have already been decided by Him."

"Yes, I have heard you are a great man of faith. I will see what I can do. There is, after all, not much time. I intend to deliver the young lady to the ship myself since she is legally in my custody. I shall call for her at ten tomorrow morning. At that time I will have your answer."

Mr. Hydemark thanked him and took his leave. He went to his home to pack his belongings before he returned to Burnside Court.

It was shortly before midnight when Bevie slipped into bed. Sleep entirely evaded her. She tossed and turned and finally decided to get up and read. She lit the lamp, put on her dressing gown, picked up her Bible, and sat next to the fire as she pulled a counterpane around herself for warmth. She couldn't concentrate and decided to walk around the house one last time. She found her guard sitting on the floor outside her door with his head hanging forward. Occasional snores escaped his open mouth. She tiptoed past him.

She went to the kitchen and picked up some apples to take with her on the ship. She thought she heard a noise at the servant's entrance and decided it must be one of the servants coming or going as they often did at night. Hearing a scuffling sound coming from outside the door, she walked into the hallway leading to the entrance. Immediately someone began pounding on the door and shouting, "Please let me in. Hurry, hurry!"

Bevie thought the voice sounded much like Suzie, her former maid. As Bevie ran toward the door, the sound of two shots filled the air. Without considering the consequences to herself, Bevie flung open the door and saw the man in the black cape running away from the house.

On further observation she saw a small figure crumpled on the ground a short distance from the doorstep. She ran to the place where the lady lay. It was Suzie and she had been shot. Bevie began screaming for help. Guards came running from all directions.

"Call for the police and the surgeon at once," Bevie ordered.

Lights began appearing in all the windows. Max was the first one of the household to arrive on the scene. His training allowed him to immediately survey the situation and take action.

"Allow me to carry her inside. Call Mrs. Metterson and ask her to bring the required supplies to stop the bleeding." He called for one of the guards. "Escort Lady Beverley to her room. There is a madman on the loose."

Bevie shook off the guard and followed Max as he carried Suzie into the small sitting room where he gently laid her on a long bench. Bevie looked down on the young lady who had once tended to her. She felt great compassion. She held her hand and disregarded the blood that was spilling over onto her own clothing.

Mrs. Metterson took over the situation and told the men to step out while she tore open Suzie's clothing to reveal a bullet hole low on her shoulder. Clean cloths were pressed onto the wound and soon filled with blood. Mrs. Metterson asked Bevie to press down on them while she tried to find a pulse on the victim.

"She is still with us, but she will not live long if we don't stop the bleeding."

Bevie pressed harder, hoping she would not break any bones. At last the bleeding seemed to slow down considerably and Mrs. Metterson took over the job. "Go to the kitchen and get some spirits and hot water from the kettle that sits over the fire," she ordered.

It seemed ages before they heard the arrival of the surgeon. He took one look at Suzie and shook his head.

Bevie kneeled down next to her and began to pray audibly. "Lord, please have mercy on this young girl and spare her life."

"Prayers are all well and good in their proper place, but we need to take action," the surgeon said through gritted teeth.

Bevie stood aside. The surgeon asked for Mrs. Metterson's assistance in removing the bullet. "It has gone deep and it is a blessing she is unconscious. I would ask everyone else to leave while we tend to this matter," he said quite emphatically, endeavoring to clear the room of nosey onlookers.

"I cannot leave her now," Bevie whispered.

"Very well, you may help hold her down if she should begin to regain her senses."

Max stood outside the room with Henry. "Step over here, Henry, I would have a private word with you," he said as they walked into the sunroom. "We have to get

Bevie out of there. It is nearly one o'clock and we were planning to accomplish our little deed at two."

"Pet has just returned. I'll have to tell her, Max. She will know exactly what to do."

"Very well, but that will make her an accomplice and the three of us may ultimately be running from the law."

"We shall deal with that another day. Excuse me while I find Pet."

Bevie refused to leave Suzie's side. The surgeon had done all he could do and left saying he would return later in the morning.

Soon after he left, another commotion took place at the front of the house when the new constable and two of his men arrived. They were led directly into the room where the victim lay and immediately began to question Bevie. Two of them left the room with instructions to search for the man in the cape. Bevie thought the order ridiculous since it was dark outside.

Max, Pet, and Henry came into the room and began demanding that Bevie be allowed to rest since she faced an ordeal in the morning. Bevie refused to leave. It was approaching the hour of two and Max was beside himself with anxiety.

Suddenly, Suzie's eyes began to flutter in the dim gas light. Bevie wiped her brow and spoke softly to her. "Wake up, dear. You are in good hands now. The danger has passed."

Suzie moaned.

The constable came near and Bevie motioned for him to back away. He stood his ground and bent over Suzie.

"I am sorry," Suzie said in such a weak voice that it was barely audible.

"Shhh, just rest now, dear," Bevie whispered.

"No, I want to tell you," Suzie uttered in a slightly stronger voice. "I didn't know it was poison."

The constable listened more intently. "Tell us more," he said rather gruffly.

"He told me it was a sleeping draught."

"Who told you?" Bevie asked.

"Hughes said it was only to put him to sleep for a while."

Bevie and the constable exchanged looks. Mrs. Metterson quickly went to find Max.

"Tell us more about it," the constable said in a softer tone so as not to disrupt the victim's words.

Suzie moaned again. She opened her eyes which were glazed over with pain. "I'm going to die, my lady. I came to tell you that I gave your father the poison. I am so sorry. Hughes made me do it. I didn't know it was poison."

"Who shot my father, Suzie?"

"Hughes shot him after he took the poison."

Max had arrived and was listening. "Well, constable, now do you see the damage your people have done here? You have convicted the wrong person," he said very angrily. Get your men down here and do whatever you have to do to take down this confession before I shoot the whole bunch of you!"

Suzie slipped back into unconsciousness. Max sent word of the confession to Lord Struthers. Henry pulled him aside and insisted they get Bevie onto Nicky's boat since the authorities had not yet discovered the source of the second bullet. "Bevie could still be charged with murder."

Suzie's pulse seemed stronger. Bevie stood up to stretch her legs. The room began to spin and she fainted.

Mrs. Metterson caught her before she hit the floor.

Max heard Mrs. Metterson's cry for help and came running back into the room. "Allow me to take charge of this situation, Max," ordered Mrs. Metterson. "Carry this poor soul to her room. She has suffered more than most of us do in a lifetime, no thanks to your people's stupid investigations," she added, glaring at the constable who was looking very sheepish.

She and Pet followed Max to Bevie's bedchamber. "Don't tuck her in bed, Max. This is perfect. Wrap her up and take her to the boat at once. The police will be occupied with Suzie and we will make excuses for Bevie's absence. You must return promptly in case we need to further the theory that Hughes has kidnapped her from under our noses."

Max did as she asked. "Help me carry her down the back stairs and out to the stables."

Pet quickly took a cloak from Bevie's dressing room and wrapped her in it. She led the way while Max hurried to get her to the stable. Henry had caught sight of them and followed close behind.

"Hold her while I saddle my horse, Henry."

Bevie began to stir as Henry lifted her up onto the horse and Max carefully held her in front of him.

"Where are we?" she asked, trying to see through the darkness.

"Never mind, just hang onto me."

"Be safe, darling," said Pet as they rode off.

"Max, are you running away with me? Wait, I cannot leave – Suzie."

"Suzie is in good hands. Just trust me, Bevie."

They sped through the night and arrived at the docks in record time. Bevie was still protesting when Max ordered her to be quiet and do as he said. Although Nicky was unaware of the events that had taken place at Burnside Court, he was awaiting her arrival since it was near the time they originally planned to deposit her there.

"She has recently fainted," Max explained, "so I will carry her on board. Is everything set?"

"Yes sir, Lord Hampden."

"There has been a slight change of plans, Nicky. Will you consider sailing around to the area near Herne Bay? Take Bevie to Whitstable. I have a good friend who owns an inn. Here is a card with the name and location. I shall endeavor to meet you there in four days time. I intend to reward you handsomely, Nicky. Have no doubt about that."

"No rewards, please, sir. Bevie is my sister's best friend. I do it for the pleasure of helping."

"You are a good man, Nicky. Take good care of her." He kissed Bevie squarely on the lips and left.

"So the man finally noticed you are a woman?" Nicky inquired with a big smile.

"He is only my protector."

"I do not think so, Bevie. I would make the duel with him, but you know I am not to get married. It would make me – how you say – in prison. So, he can have you. He is the marry-kind of man."

Bevie laughed, thinking him slightly mad. They were already moving toward the sea and Bevie had no idea how everything had changed so quickly. Somehow, she felt that it had all happened exactly the way it was meant to turn out. She breathed a prayer of thanks and one for Suzie's recovery.

Mr. Hydemark returned to the house to find it in chaos. Mrs. Metterson took him aside and explained the circumstances surrounding the latest events.

"I am very sorry to go against your wishes, Mr. Hydemark, but we all thought it was best for Bevie to escape when the opportunity presented itself. After all, you know she is as innocent as a new-born babe."

"I suppose you had to do what you did, but I cannot like it. I will pray that it comes about without repercussions, Mina."

"You have said on more than one occasion that there are times when God's will supersedes the law of the land, Mr. Hydemark."

"So I have – so I have."

Max slipped quietly into the room where Suzie lay. Mrs. Jackson had taken over the nursing duties. "We should move her to a comfortable bed," he said.

"The surgeon said not to move her until he sees her later this morning."

"That is most likely the best thing. Has she spoken again?"

"No, but she has awakened briefly. I am beginning to think she will live."

"Please send for me if she awakens. There are a few more things I wish to know. I am sending some guards to surround her. I fear Hughes may return to finish the job."

CHAPTER SEVENTEEN

They moved Suzie to a comfortable bed while the surgeon attended her and assured her caretakers that the bleeding had stopped. Max and Mrs. Jackson sat by her bed and assured her that Hughes could not penetrate the number of guards who were stationed at intervals around the property.

"You are too good to me, my lord. I deserve to die."

"It was not your fault, Suzie, but I am curious to know how you got mixed up in this terrible thing."

"I am ashamed to say, my lord," she said, her eyes darting back and forth between Mrs. Jackson and Max.

Max nodded to Mrs. Jackson. She graciously left the room.

A tear ran down Suzie's cheek. "At first he treated me like a queen – bought me little things 'n all. I had an affair with him and soon after that, he threatened to have me sent off without a character if I did not do what he wanted, my lord. I swear I did not know it was poison he put in Lord Burnside's coffee. He said it would only put the gent to sleep so he could have a look at his books."

"Did you realize, Suzie, that bullets from two different guns were found in Burnside's body? It means that another person shot Lord Burnside in addition to Hughes. Do you know who that person is?"

Suzie hesitated for a moment. "It were that awful mother of the red-haired man. She shot him after he were done in – stupid woman. Hughes saw her do it and told me. She shot 'im and the bullet went through the glass – a right good aim she was."

"I see, so Mrs. Busslingthorpe shot him?"

"That's what Hughes told me."

"Are you willing to tell this to the authorities, Suzie?"

"Alright, but I don't want no more trouble from Hughes. He near done me in, too."

When Pet and Henry heard the news of Suzie's confession, they happily went ahead with their plans for a wedding. Pet confessed to Henry that she had become quite wealthy due to an inheritance from her father's uncle who had often taken care of her while her parents were traveling. "He left Nicky and I well-off. He was very much against my parents leaving us with various people during most of our childhood. He really did love us."

"I had no idea I was about to marry an heiress. Oh well, it is just as well since I have very few coins to rub together and little in the bank to account for."

"I wouldn't care if you were a pauper, my darling. It is only your acumen with numbers that attracted me." She laughed and reached up to kiss him.

Lord Struthers developed a stern frown when Max confessed that he had sent Bevie away before all the legal entanglements regarding her release had been sorted out.

Lord Struthers laughed and said that Max was just like his father who, in fact, would have done exactly the same. "She's a lovely girl, Max. Your father would have wanted you to settle and I am certain your mother looks forward to the day when you present her with a grandchild. What about it, lad?"

Bevie was cleared of any wrong-doing and Max took his phaeton to Whitstable where he found her ensconced in a comfortable room at his friend's inn. He profusely thanked Nicky who refused to take the money Max offered. Max and Bevie stood on the dock waving to Nicky as he sailed off toward France. He promised to be back in time for Pet's wedding.

The weather was fine for the ride home. Max and Bevie discussed the horrors of recent weeks.

Max looked thoughtfully at Bevie. "I don't know exactly what to do about Suzie now that she is recuperating. I still fear for her safety where Hughes is concerned, but I cannot countenance having her stay at Burnside Court after what she has done. The other servants would likely make it impossible for her to live in peace."

"I agree. I had warned her to stay away from the man she was seeing, but I had no idea it was Hughes. Although I do forgive her, I must admit to feeling a bit angry that she went on with that ill-fated affair."

"I believe I shall send her off to my cousin's place in the country. No one knows her there and she can fade into the background. Let us hope and pray that Hughes is soon caught."

Bevie sighed. "Now I shall settle into a more sedate lifestyle and you are free to go back to your life, Max. I am going to miss you terribly. I confess I have come to lean very hard on you for everything."

"It is time for you to have a season, Bevie."

"I could never. Firstly, I am in mourning. Secondly, the *ton* has already pronounced me guilty of murder and I would be ostracized. Surely you must understand that, Max. At any rate, I have no wish to partake in their useless parties and balls. Oh, look! There is a lovely little inn just ahead. May we stop for tea?"

They sat by the window and leisurely sipped their tea.

"What would you like to do now, Bevie? I must go north to see about my own family business. When I return, we shall decide what is best for you."

"Please take me with you, Max."

Bevie observed the shocked look on his face. "I believe heads would turn and you would become the object of many rumors, my sweet."

Bevie laughed. "I suppose you are going to tell me that I have not been the object of scorn for the past few weeks. I care nothing for the *ton's* attitude toward me, but I have to say that I wonder what your attitude might be."

"I think you know, minx. I am not exactly immune to your charms and perhaps it is best if I leave someone else to oversee Burnside Court."

Bevie put her head down. "I suppose I have been a pest. Perhaps in a year or two you would reconsider."

"What am I to reconsider?"

"Don't act stupid, Max. You know exactly what I mean. In fact, when Nicky saw you kissing me, he said that you had finally realized that I am a woman. I am, you see."

Max laughed. "Oh, I have very little doubt about it, my sweet, but lean toward me so that I can be certain."

"Right here – in front of these people? How shaming," she said as their lips met over the plate of tea sandwiches.

"You have passed the test," he said, laughing. "Shall we proceed on our way home?" He left money on the table and retrieved their wraps.

Bevie was confused. She had no idea what his feelings were for her. On the other hand, she decided at that moment that she wanted to marry him, only he apparently had no such thing in mind. She forced herself to focus on the fact that she was now free to pursue the life she had always imagined.

They bounced along in the phaeton without speaking. A half hour later the weather began to deteriorate. "Perhaps it was foolish to bring the phaeton," Max said distractedly. "We still have a distance to travel."

"I am not so missish as to mind some inclement weather," she answered defensively.

He looked at her with an amused twinkle in his brown eyes. "No, I do not suppose you are. The weather must seem very unimportant to you after all that you have suffered lately."

"Why won't you allow me to come with you to your family home, Max? I promise to be very well-behaved and proper. I haven't had much of an opportunity to be away from Burnside Court since I returned from Switzerland." After she spoke the words, she could not imagine what had come over her to cause her to be so brazen.

"I have already explained the situation to you, my dear. It would stir up the bramblebroth to where it would overflow the pot. Need I mention that the *ton* is already on high alert concerning your reputation?"

Bevie was not one to pout as did most of the debutantes in her circles. She suddenly felt ashamed that she had forced the issue with Max and realized he had no romantic interest in her and had only flirted a little.

"You are quite right, my lord, and I cannot imagine what came over me to suggest such a dim-witted idea. There is one thing I would ask of you."

"Anything that is in my power to do, my dear."

"At this point, I have no idea how tightly you will hold the reins of the Burnside fortunes and I wonder if you would release enough funds for me to travel on the Continent. It is something I have always wanted to do."

"There again, my love, it would not be the thing. It is considered highly improper for a single young lady of consequence to travel alone."

"I would have a companion, of course."

"Who?"

"I am not certain, but I will look into the matter."

The phaeton swerved and rocked violently. Max reined in the horses and brought them to a stop. "Poor fellow has tossed a shoe. We will have to stop here. Fortunately, we are very near a village. Come along, my sweet. You'll have to ride the other horse and I will lead this fine fellow to the blacksmith shop."

Max unhitched the horses and they slowly made their way toward the village of Ashton Wells.

"I will reserve a room at the inn. You may rest there while I tend to the horses."

A short while later, Max tapped on her door and entered the room. "They are short of staff today and we shall be required to dine in the main dining hall. I hope the food is better than the service."

The food was placed on the table. Bevie began to sample the dishes and had no complaints. Max did not agree. "This is the worst lamb I have ever eaten."

"Perhaps you should try prison food, my lord. This food is fit for the kings compared to what I was forced to eat in that place."

Max felt ashamed. "I am so sorry you had to endure such dreadful treatment, my love."

"Stop calling me your love. I am not your love," she said rather vehemently.

"Shall I apologize for that as well?"

Bevie could not fathom what came over her. She began to cry.

"What have I done? I didn't mean to. . . I told you when we first met that I have no idea how to handle tears." He ignored the rest of the company in the dining room and suddenly pushed away from the table, picked up Bevie from her chair, and set her on his lap. She put her head on his shoulder and sobbed. He patted her back and kissed her forehead.

"Excuse me, Max old boy. I hope I am not interrupting a private moment," said a tall man who had just entered the dining room. He stood behind Max, removed his beaver hat and bowed.

"Oh, hello Crandall. What brings you here?" replied an extremely annoyed Max.

"Might I inquire the same of you, sir?" the man inquired with a sneer.

Two ladies walked up and stood behind Crandall. He did not bother to introduce them. From the looks of their attire, Max knew they were not the kind of women one would introduce to quality friends.

"I see we have the same thing in mind, Max. Who is this raving beauty? Anyone I should know?"

"Not if I have anything to say about it, Crandall. She is my ward and is just now in deep mourning for her father. The decent thing would be for you to leave us now and pursue your – er – activities elsewhere."

"Oh, certainly, St. Ives," he said with a sly laugh. "Far be it from me to disturb you." He bowed again and took the two girls in hand and left the room.

Max set Bevie back in her chair, sat down, and put his head in his hands.

"Is it that bad, Max?"

"Yes, I am afraid it is. Crandall is a nasty piece of work and the worst gossip this side of the channel."

"Do not regard it, Max. My reputation is of no consequence. Let him say what he pleases. This is one more reason for you to allow me to travel on the Continent."

"You don't understand, do you? I have just now ruined you! I can never forgive myself."

Bevie was ambivalent. She had no fear of the *ton*. Others had done much worse and lived through it. "I do understand, Max, but I do not care. Can you not understand that?"

"Well, I do care – and deeply."

"For my reputation or your own?"

He picked her up and set her on his lap again. "Don't be a goose, my love. You wouldn't consider marrying an old coot like me, would you?"

"Not if you are asking simply for the purpose of saving me from the tongues of the *ton*."

"Would unreasonably mad love be a proper reason?"

"Yes, I believe it would. In that case, my answer is yes – a hundred times, yes."

"Then come away with me, my beauty. My mother will wish to meet you. We will return in time for Pet's wedding and then we shall plan our own."

The serving girl stood aside smiling as the two left the inn. Max's arm tightened around the small waist of his intended. They had a new subject to discuss as they slowly made their way back to Burnside Court.

"There is one thing, Max. I must insist that Mr. Hydemark act in the place of my father at our wedding. He has become very important to me and I wish to have him by my side to help me when I am struggling with life's problems. Do you realize he is a great man of God?"

"I can only agree to your spending time with him if you promise to leave him behind when we embark on our wedding trip to the Continent."

"Of course, you big goose. Wait, I have a splendid idea. Do you think Pet and Henry would consider a double wedding?"

"Why is it that I have the feeling you and Pet planned a double wedding from the time you first knew each other?"

"The answer to that, my darling man, is a secret I shall never reveal."

"Now I am worried about what else the two of you have planned."

Bevie decided to pay the respect due her father and wait until a proper period of mourning had passed before she wed. Pet insisted on delaying her own nuptials until Bevie was ready to speak her vows. Naturally, the two couples were joined in holy matrimony at St. George's Chapel where the two young women had, years before, made secret plans to have a double wedding. Many of the uninvited *haute ton* stood outside the chapel waiting for the brides to appear.

The wedding breakfast took place at Burnside Court where the guests included most of the staff. Sixteen guards split into two groups. One group guarded the grounds while the other joined in the festivities. After a time, they switched places.

William sulked as he watched the wedding party leave the house. He called on several of his hunting friends before he went speedily to his father's newly inherited hunting lodge with the excuse that he needed to make certain everything was ready for the upcoming season.

On returning from their wedding trip, Bevie was distressed to find a new housekeeper in place. She entered the library in a flutter and stood with her hands on her hips demanding attention. "My Lord Hampden, what have you done with Mrs. Jackson?"

"Well, saucy lady, I have pensioned her off and set her up in the Southfork Cottage in hopes that she will occasionally look in on her next-door neighbor, Mr. Hornsby."

"You can't mean that dear old gardener. Have you gotten rid of him as well?"

"My dear wife, they are both too old to work so hard. I believe he is approaching his seventy-sixth year."

"Oh, I had no idea." She walked to the desk and sat on her husband's lap. "You, my dear Lord Hampden, are a wonder."

Araminta Busslingthorpe was found guilty of attempted murder and speedily deported. Lady Mary refused to listen to Cecil's excuses for his mother's abominable behavior and decided to marry the grandson of a duke. Cecil pleaded innocent before the court wherein the charges were dismissed. He planned to join Her Majesty's Service in whatever capacity he was able to secure a position.

Franklin was released from prison and sought remuneration from Cecil and Araminta for taking the trouble to whisper a lie in Constable Green's ear concerning the gun that had been placed in Bevie's room. Max offered him the choice of leaving the country on his own or finding himself chained in the hold of a ship bound for Australia.

Constable Green gazed out the window of his make-shift office on the tiny island off the coast of Scotland. He truly wished he had never laid eyes on Lady Beverley.

Suzie worked as an upstairs maid at the grand country manor of one of Max's cousins. Some months later, Hughes was spotted in the North of England by Mr. Hydemark who, along with Mrs. Metterson, was helping another genteel young lady in that vicinity to weather the storms of life. Hughes was taken into custody and forced to stand trial. He was found guilty of murder.

Bevie and Pet had never actually planned for their babies to be born on the same day. However, one year after they had spoken their vows, God saw fit to bless them again. They sat side-by-side in front of the hearth in the townhouse of a very proud Uncle Nicky and laughed at their tiny sons. Max and Henry stood in the doorway gazing fondly at their wives and wondering how they had managed to plan such an extraordinary event.

www.ingramcontent.com/pod-product-compliance
Lightning Source LLC
Chambersburg PA
CBHW070440120726
47910CB00003B/859